Richard Dadd in Bedlam and Other Stories

Alan Wall was born in Bradford in the West Riding of Yorkshire, and was educated there and at Pembroke College, Oxford. He is married with three children and lives in London.

Also by Alan Wall

JACOB

CURVED LIGHT

CHRONICLE

BLESS THE THIEF

LENSES

A TO Z

SILENT CONVERSATIONS

Richard Dadd in Bedlam and Other Stories

ALAN WALL

Secker & Warburg
London

Published by Secker & Warburg 1999

2 4 6 8 10 9 7 5 3 1

Copyright © 1999 by Alan Wall

First published in Great Britain in 1999 by Secker & Warburg
Random House, 20 Vauxhall Bridge Road,
London SW1V 2SA

Random House Australia (Pty) Limited
20 Alfred Street, Milsons Point, Sydney,
New South Wales 2061, Australia

Random House New Zealand Limited
18 Poland Road, Glenfield,
Auckland 10, New Zealand

Random House South Africa (Pty) Limited
Endulini, 5A Jubilee Road,
Parktown 2193, South Africa

Random House UK Limited Reg. No. 954009

A CIP catalogue record for this book
is available from the British Library

ISBN 0 436 22080 6

Papers used by Random House UK Limited are natural,
recyclable products made from wood grown in sustainable forests.
The manufacturing processes conform to the environmental
regulations of the country of origin.

Typeset by Deltatype Ltd, Birkenhead, Merseyside
Printed and bound in Great Britain by
Creative Print and Design (Wales), Ebbw Vale

Contents

Acknowledgments

I would like to thank the following for their help: Philip Byrne, Gill Coleridge, Marius Kociejowski, Elena Lappin, Ray Leach, Geoff Mulligan, David Rees, Nathaniel and Anthony Rudolf and Lucy Winward.

'Doctor Freud and Mister Looney' was first published in the *Jewish Quarterly*; 'Logical Positivists' in the *London Magazine*; 'A to Z' was brought out as a limited edition by Colophon Press.

A to Z

My name's Harry Selbourne and I'd rather not be telling this story, but now that all the reports are in, the newspaper articles printed and the bodies shovelled underground, there's something missing. And if I don't write it down it'll stay missing for ever.

I wanted out and I'd wanted out for a long time. I'd seen enough mangled faces and punctured torsos to last me a lifetime. So when they privatised the force I made my pitch for Research Section K, the end-of-the-world brigade as my colleagues call it. And I got it. Got out of London too. Back to my beloved West Riding. Since we'd managed to have Yorkshire restored to its ancient nomenclature, though no thanks to our revered leaders, and since Leningrad was now St Petersburg again, I sometimes wondered if maybe the end of the world might be coming round after all.

Some people certainly thought so, and had some unsociable ways of trying to prove the point. The bombings, the gassings, the executions, the kidnappings, the hijacks. Cryptic notes would arrive and it was my job to fathom out what particular brand of maniac we were dealing with. This had meant a lot of reading, for I was the one they called the apocalypse boy. From the Book of Revelation to Joachim of Fiore, from Jim Jones to the Japanese Aum cult, I kept my archives up to date.

Everything was on a computer now. Communication was screen to screen not door to door. No need for me to leave my little house in Baildon, except to take a walk on the moors or buy a loaf. I'd set things up exactly as I would have wished. Still technically employed by the Metropolitan Police, I lived two hundred and fifty miles away from all of it. And after the millennium itself, it was all growing worse, much worse. When the year 2000 came and went, and the human race was still about its sordid business, the millennialists grew even more frantic than before. Now it was every man for himself – and every woman too, of course, it goes without saying, though men still seemed to take the lead in slaughter. There's one aspect of history, at least, which hasn't changed much.

Now the problem with Everyman reading his way through the Bible is that he tends to start at the beginning again each time. And the beginning is his own life, his own death, his own disappointments. Sooner or later he finds himself with the Book of Daniel or the Book of Revelation in his lap and his imagination goes into overdrive. All those old theologians spent half their lives saying, Slow down, Everyman, take it easy: things don't necessarily mean exactly what you'd like to think they mean. As far as I could see, this was true from Augustine onwards: if you give the game to the Gnostics, you can believe whatever you like. Darkness and light are at your disposal, and tradition is no more than what you were thinking an hour ago. Well, there was no Augustine around now, or, if there was, I hadn't been given his e-mail address.

I read my books, I took my walks, I told the boys down in the smoke what I thought their messages might mean. And this suited me fine.

You can imagine then my initial reaction when this message came on to my screen:

Depart for London immediately.

Body found in mysterious circumstances.

Cult killing suspected.

I was on the phone a minute later to Frank Scully.

'What's all this, Frank? Why do I suddenly have to come and contaminate myself with London air? Why can't I work from home the way I always do?'

'Something funny about this one, Harry.'

'What have you got?'

'Twenty-five-year-old. Caucasian female. Massive overdose of heroin. Body dressed in a long white muslin shift dumped in Leinster Gardens.'

'So?'

'On her right palm a tattoo of a horseshoe. Pathologist says the tattoo was applied a matter of hours before death.'

'You said Leinster Gardens?'

'Yes.'

'One of the girls?'

'We think. Collared a couple of others on the street and showed them the picture. They said they'd seen her out there.'

'Actually seen her on the game?'

'They said.'

'Still don't see what all the fuss is about, Frank. Some tom cops it with an extra helping of smack and says goodnight in her usual working environment. Maybe she fancied one last tattoo before going to meet her Maker.'

'There's something else, Harry. Which is why you're getting called in. On the muslin shift was embroidered . . .'

'Embroidered?'

'As I said, embroidered, Rev 1.11. Mean anything?'

'Revelation chapter one, verse eleven. Hang on,' I said, 'let me get my Bible.' I took it down from the shelf and read it out over the phone. 'Saying, I am Alpha and Omega, the first and the last. OK, so we've got an end-time stiff on our hands. I still don't see why I have to leave the peace and quiet of the Yorkshire moors to see your ugly mug again. Last week, sweetheart, in case you've forgotten, seven children went up in smoke in your Deptford case. Nobody asked me to come to London then.'

'Hang on, Harry, I think I may have the answer for you. Just coming up on the screen, a positive ID. The name's Sarah Tinley.'

'Tinley. No relation, I trust, to . . .'

'You trust wrong, Harry. Daughter of one Sir James Tinley.'

'The Commissioner of Police.'

'That's the fellow.'

'I'll pack my bag then. See you there tonight.'

Maybe it's that I'm older and fatter. At fifty-one I don't feel like looking the world in the eye any more. I'd prefer the world to leave me alone altogether. I'm happy to be left with my books. Who was that American who said, 'Some people say that life's the thing, but I prefer reading'? He has my vote, anyway.

The trip to London was a nightmare from the ticket office onwards. You can never be sure beforehand if one sector is going to be as enthusiastic at signalling you through as the next. And all the way down those eyes and voices. Were they always so loud? Even the eyes are loud now.

I took a taxi from King's Cross straight to the new morgue in Vauxhall. Frank was in the atrium, stroking the leaves of an artificial palm tree.

'Good to have you back with us, Harry.'

'Wish I could say the same.'

'You've put on weight.'

'Fish and chips and Tetley's bitter.'

'We'll soon have that off you.'

'I imagine you will at that.'

As we approached Room D11, the Commissioner appeared with his weeping wife. Frank introduced us.

'Commissioner Tinley, this is Harry Selbourne, he's handling data on this case.'

The Commissioner looked at me as only someone who's in charge can look at someone who's not.

'Any other work on, Detective-Sergeant?'

'Left it all at home, sir.'

'Good man. I want the swiftest possible results.'

'Understood, sir.'

He went off down the corridor, arm around the missus.

'You can forget about your Deptford case for a while then, Frank.'

'Won't bring 'em back anyway,' he said.

'Not expecting me to actually bring this one back, are you?'

'If you could manage it, there'd probably be a sizeable bonus for you.'

The white-suited attendant took us to the steel drawer. He hadn't even closed it yet, after the parents had paid their last respects. I was surprised. She was pretty, nothing ravaged about her, no emaciation. Hair still done back nicely in a bun. Fine cheekbones. In fact more than pretty, that wasn't the right word at all. I'd been expecting a junkie.

'Where's the tattoo then?' I asked.

He opened out the girl's right palm. There it was, the flesh still a little inflamed from the recent triggering of the needle.

'Why a horseshoe?' he asked.

6

'I don't think that is a horseshoe, I'd say it's an omega.'

'Don't stop now, Harry.'

'The last letter of the Greek alphabet. Often used as a symbol of the end of time. God himself is the alpha and omega, remember. I read it out to you. Show me the shift,' I said.

The attendant went to a drawer and pulled it out. I held it up against Frank.

'It's a bit small for me, Harry. I take a size sixteen.'

'Revelation chapter one, verse eleven,' I said. 'Saying, I am Alpha and Omega, the first and the last. And what's this above it? A number 1. Where was the injection?'

'In the right wrist.'

'Above the tattoo?'

'Yes.'

'Can I have a look?'

The attendant held out the lady's hand for me. A clean mark, nothing ragged about it.

'She a user then?'

'Not as far as we can see. No marks on her anywhere.'

'Quite a big sachet for her first prick at the balloon, wasn't it? And you say she was on the game?'

'The girls have seen her round there. Saw her go off with a man in a car.'

'What's the Commissioner got to say about that?'

'No one's mentioned it to him yet, funnily enough. We thought we'd let you handle that one. Fresh-faced country boy, new to the city.'

'Thanks, friend.'

There was something odd. There always is in the apocalypse department, but this was different. One thing thirty-three years as a copper have taught me: trust your instincts. Whenever I don't, I go wrong. I've seen enough dead whores in my time to know what they look like. Some still look pretty, though hard with it usually; some have been ravaged by their life on the streets, the beatings, the needles, the abortions. They don't look like her, though. Never seen a tom alive or dead who looked like Miss Sarah Tinley. And when people have been killed, the ghost of a rictus stays in the corpse's face to haunt it. The violence is still in there screaming at you. Silently screaming. Her face wasn't like that. Sarah was smiling. She looked as though her true love had arrived at last, as though she'd just heard the last line of the fairy tale.

The house in Holland Park was big, with a twenty-foot cast-iron canopy leading up its steps. I didn't know Police Commissioners made that kind of money. Maybe his wife had inherited. Inside I decided in favour of the wife. Too many Impressionist paintings, too many antique chairs. Coppers, even top coppers, wouldn't spend all their pennies on that sort of stuff. This lady had a rich dead daddy.

They were cut up, though, there was no doubt about that. I can tell the difference between grief and inconvenience, and this one was twenty-four-carat grief.

'You won't take liquor I assume?'

'Never on duty sir, no. Tea would be nice.'

We sat in a living room the size of my house and garden. You'd have to employ a lot of people to keep a place so big as tidy as that. Or else live somewhere different for fifty weeks of the year. I felt that I was littering, just by landing my crumpled bulk on one of the Regency chairs.

'I'm sorry to have to ask questions at such a time . . .'

'Get on with it, man,' snapped Commissioner Tinley. That wasn't his grief speaking either.

'Yes, sir. Your daughter is . . . or rather was single. Any boyfriends?'

'Not that we know of,' he said. I took a sip of tea.

'Girlfriend?'

The Commissioner looked at me and shook his head slowly from side to side. He put his arm around his wife again. She was snuffling into a handkerchief.

'I have to ask, sir.'

'I understand.'

'What did your daughter do for a living?'

'She was working on a PhD.'

'At?'

'Quentin College in Roehampton. Affiliated to the University of London.'

'So she lived on a grant?'

'No,' he said, taking his arm away from his wife again. 'No, we provided all the money she needed.'

'Where did she live, sir? At the address provided here on my printout? Nevern Square, off the Earls Court.'

9

Alan Wall

'Yes. We bought her the flat for her twenty-first. Though the location, I should say, was her own choice.'

'I was planning on going to examine the place after I leave here.'

'Obviously.'

'I have a question, sir, you may perhaps find offensive; but I have to do my job, as you of all people understand.'

'I already told you to get on with it.'

I finished my tea, breathed in and looked down at the printout.

'It is claimed that your daughter was involved in prostitution.'

At this the Commissioner's wife stood up and stared at me with undisguised loathing. She was still sobbing.

'Let me know when this . . . man of yours has left, will you, James?' She walked out of the room.

'Sorry, sir.'

'Who says this?' he said, starting to become angry for the first time. 'Who?'

'The girls on the game in Paddington say she's been seen soliciting up there and has left the street with men. Or at least with one man.'

'Most reliable witnesses, obviously.'

'All the same, it's hard to imagine why they'd lie, sir.'

'To get the filth off their back before the next punter arrives, possibly?'

'I think our investigators might have been a little more subtle than that.'

'Will this get into the papers then?'

'Not through me it won't.'

'There's more than you who know, though.'

'There's more than me who know, that's true.'

'Then it will.'

'Perhaps you could use your influence in some way to . . .'

'No. Out of the question. You must proceed as you would normally,' he said and stood up. 'Any more questions?'

'Only one, sir. Did your daughter have any particular interest in Christianity, and in particular the Book of Revelation?'

'I sometimes think it's the only thing she *did* have any interest in,' he said wearily and opened the door. I was being shown out.

The squad car was waiting for me as requested. As it set off towards Nevern Square I went through the faxed bank statements the driver handed me. Miss Tinley was an exemplary citizen, so it seemed. She received her twenty grand yearly from mummy and daddy's joint account, took five hundred a month out, paid her bills by standing order, and that was it. This wasn't someone on drugs, and it wasn't anyone who needed to go on the game either. Smack and the street don't make for such regular book-keeping.

Earls Court was choked up with traffic. I told the driver to give me the keys to the flat and blue-light it off into the night.

'Know the way do you, sir?'

'I have my *A to Z*. Never visit your beautiful city without it.'

But I didn't need an *A to Z* to find my way to Nevern Square. Spent too much time on these streets in a previous incarnation. Earls Court hadn't changed much. Dead meals scattered over the pavement. Dead chips. Dead curries. Dead kebabs. It's a multi-ethnic gastronomic morgue, the second morgue I'd been in during the last two hours. How far away Baildon seemed already.

113 Nevern Square was like all the others. And Flat Nine was on the top floor. No lift. I realised I was going to have to lose some weight because by the time I was up there I was sweating and panting. On the way I noticed the piece of ragged paper with **Fierce Dog** scrawled on it in pencil on one door and **Be Loved Within** on another. I shoved the keys into the lock and wheezed inside.

Sarah was a tidy girl. Nothing out of place. Some books and papers on the desk. Clothes neatly hooked. A drinks table, but our girl was no drinker. A couple of thimbles had been taken out of the whisky, the gin and the sherry. She was what I'd call a Christmas drinker. I'm not. So I poured myself a whisky. I lied to the Commissioner, by the way: I do sometimes drink while working, but I try to avoid it in front of my superior officers.

I wandered about, sipping the Scotch. I'm not sure what people mean by the extra-sensory. I know what I mean by my instincts, though. I've been in rooms where I could sense the violence, the fear, the terror; rooms where I could tell from the mere smell of them that someone was going to die there, if not sooner then later. Rooms where I could hear the sobs of the child with the sheets pulled over her head as the footsteps came closer. But not here. This was pure serenity. I wanted to stay here. I wanted to meet the person who could perfume the air of London like this, but I was already too late by about twenty hours.

I helped myself to another whisky and took the black notebook from her desk. Inside the front cover it said *Figurae* above her name. Inside were dated entries, the last one being the 3rd, the day of her death. It read as follows:

Look at what is before you. Nothing is accidental.
His name completes the saeculum. He must die last.

The boys had already been over and done their fingerprinting. I put the notebook in my bag, then I went to the table and took a photograph of our girl, still in its frame, and placed that carefully in the bag too.

They had booked me at my own request into the Zorba Hotel on Craven Hill. I wanted to be near to the field of my study. I had requested the two connecting rooms at the top of the building because I wanted to keep my sleeping and washing arrangements separate from my work, and I knew that I might well be doing some late-night interviewing. I knew the Zorba. I even knew the original flea-bitten Greek who'd blessed the place with its moniker, but he'd long ago gone to take his place in the pantheon. God alone knew who owned it now.

A snot, I was to find out shortly, after my taxi flipped me on to the befouled pavement. One of the classic products of our time: university educated, unemployable, unendurable. When the parents finally shuffle off this mortal coil, and bequeath their bundle, it's a small hotel in London or a restaurant in Cornwall. Not that either normally lasts for long. Then after that, indigence, and a ceaseless whingeing about the failings of state support. This boy was destined to become part of the growing army of over-qualified mendicants.

'I'm not used to having my rooms requisitioned by the police,' he said.

'Anybody in them, is there?'

'No,' he said, 'but that's not the point. I normally decide which rooms my guests will have. That's if I decide they're suitable clientèle in the first place.'

I waved my badge under his nose.

'Detective-Sergeant Selbourne,' I said. 'On a very important murder inquiry. You can be of some assistance to us if you choose. But it's not a legal obligation,' I said. 'So tell me to bugger off if you like, and I'll go find myself another maggot-bag to kip in. Of course you may find my friends the rat-finders pop round by the end of the week. And I do know a few people in VAT and Revenue. But then I'm sure your books are as immaculate as your kitchens, aren't they, sunshine.'

He handed me both sets of keys.

'Am I alone on the floor?'

'Yes,' he said, looking at his register. I turned it round so I could read it.

'Well, blow me down with a feather,' I said, 'it looks as though I'm alone in the building too. Bad season is it? Or are you only renting by the hour these days? Maybe your desk manners have something to do with it. Don't put anyone else on the top floor and don't put anyone else immediately beneath me. I want to come and go as I please and no complaints. So let's just get a few things straight, shall we . . .'

'Ashburton,' he said, 'the name's Ashburton. Mr Ashburton to you. Or you can call me sir if you find it easier.'

'Right then, *Mister* Ashburton,' I said, with the contempt every policeman knows how to employ when using someone's name, 'let's get it all clear now, shall we? I don't want to be in your fifth-rate little doss-house any longer than you want me to be here. So the sooner I can get my job finished and be off, the better for both of us.

'I may be bringing people back late at night to talk. The sort of people you can only get to talk to when it's dark, because that's when they work.'

'Wear skirts do they, these people?'

'Yes. And with me they'll be keeping them on.'

'If you say so. Wife crossed her legs on you has she?'

'Don't you cross me, Mr Ashburton. And don't you ever mention my family again.'

I climbed the stairs. Seventy of them. No lift. I'm a real

martyr to my vocation, aren't I? But I still remembered the window. From there you could look down and see the streets where the girls started their tours. I'd been here before. Last time it cost a Foreign Minister his job. Only a job though. This time it was a life, a very special life, as I'd already come to think. Don't let anyone tell you coppers don't get involved in their cases. I was in love with Sarah before she was twenty-four hours dead.

I put my pyjamas under my pillow and my toothbrush, toothpaste and mouthwash on the sink. That was one room arranged. Then I took out the bottle of Scotch that I'd bought on the way, and then Sarah's photograph and notebook, and I went through to my workroom, library and interviewing chamber by the connecting door. I pulled the table over to the window so that I could sit there and read and think, and see when the ladies of the night slipped out to take a little southern air.

I put Sarah's photograph on the table facing me and her notebook in front of me, along with the laptop computer. And at the back of the table I placed the King James Bible in its battered green leather binding. Inside it said *Harry Selbourne, for Exemplary Scriptural Knowledge, 1960.*

Mr Ashburton had rattled me, if the truth be told. It's always a mistake to make jokes about a man's sex life with his wife, simply because so many of us don't have one any more. It's not difficult to touch a sore point with us there since we already happen to be sore all over. My wife left with my son twelve years ago, and I never have worked out whose fault it was (some detective, aren't I?). She said mine: police work, nightly fatigue, never spoke to her about anything of any importance, and so on and so forth. I said, I only did all the extra work for you and the boy. I was barely allowed to touch her after she'd got pregnant. Might as well have stayed single. I did love my son, though, and I still do. I didn't want him taken away from me, but the courts had other ideas. And who am I, when all's said and done, to go round criticising the law? But I'll get Ashburton for that merry little quip, you see if I don't. Before I leave here, I'll find his wound and put a rusty syringe in it for him. And then I'll do him on suspicion of using illegal substances. The dignity of the constabulary must be upheld.

I made a note to buy some new glasses. The thick, chipped, false-teeth containers that hang in a silver ring on the bathroom wall in these places seem designed to stop you drinking altogether. I persevered, though, and started to key in some initial data on to the laptop. None of it made any sense at all. The strangest thing, stranger than all the other oddities, was that I couldn't get my own instincts to accept that Sarah had been murdered. That she was dead was indisputable, but murdered? I didn't know what to make of this.

Around ten the girls started to appear in their party frocks and their cleavage doilies. For a minute I almost felt the old Adam rising, then I remembered I had work to do. And when I was an old lag on this beat, who were the punters I thought the most pathetic ones of all? Overweight men in their early fifties whose wives didn't understand them. No, I'd already felt enough contempt for myself to last one lifetime. If I could only get it by paying for it, then I'd do without.

I slipped the photograph of Sarah into my jacket pocket, finished the Scotch in the glass, unfastened the hotel key from its wooden number plaque and set off down the stairs. At the bottom our intellectual was sitting behind his counter reading the *TLS*.

'Key, please,' he said, holding out his hand without looking up.

'I'll keep it,' I said. 'Don't know when I'll be back.'

'You will make yourself at home, won't you?' he said, still not looking up.

'I'll try,' I said, 'but you and I probably have a different idea of what the word means.'

It was a warm night. I could remember the circuit well enough. Up Craven Hill, then down to the bottom of Leinster Gardens until you hit Cleveland. They'd found Sarah down there. Someone might well have seen her body being dumped, but maybe they were too far on the wrong side of the law themselves to bother mentioning the fact.

They adopted either a brisk pace or a provocative dawdle, eyes alert to the merest possibility that there might be a desire to be quenched for hard cash. A few half-started with their 'Want some business, darling?', but something about my manner made them stop. Despite my years in Yorkshire there was still enough of the policeman in me to alert them. I have my instincts, and they have theirs.

Near the bottom of Queensborough I saw Shirley. I had wondered if she'd still be out there working.

'Hello, Shirley, remember me?'

She stared for a moment under the street light.

'Well, I never. Detective Selbourne. You look older.'

'Detective-Sergeant, Shirley. And I'm not sure the years have been too kind to either of us.' That was a stupid thing to say, wasn't it? Why did I have to go and say that? Particularly since it was true. All those tiny spidermarks across her skin. The mirror said bad enough things to her every morning, so who'd employed me to join the chorus?

'Well thanks, you always were the gallant gentleman.'

'Sorry, Shirley. You look fine actually. I'm still a little bit vain myself, you know.'

'You're a man,' she said, 'so I was taking that for granted.'

I had a feeling life on the streets couldn't be too easy for Shirley any more. Men who are paying for sex all seem to have 20:20 vision. There's probably a long waiting list to join Call-Girls for the Blind.

'Come back to my hotel, Shirley, just up the road on Craven Hill. I'll give you thirty and you can have a Scotch as well.'

'It's fifty now, Harry. You have been away a long time.'

'I only want to ask you some questions.'

'Whatever turns you on, darling, you always were the

talkative type, but if you want me to step off the street with you, it's fifty.'

'Half an hour.'

'Twenty minutes.'

'I thought the story these days was that you were providing a social service.'

'If we are, shouldn't you tell your friends to stop arresting us?'

'They're not my friends.'

'Well, they're certainly not mine.'

We arrived at the hotel. Lord Snot was still reading his supplement behind the desk as I led Shirley to the stairs.

'Care to check in, Mrs Selbourne?' he said. Shirley looked at me to find out what to do. I walked over to the desk and leaned across it.

'I've told you to watch it, *Mister* Ashburton. Now mind your lip, son, or I'll have you. I will, you know.'

'You must be desperate tonight, Shirley,' he said, and turned back to his paper.

'I'm going to put my foot on that cockroach before I leave here.'

'Put your other foot on him for me while you're at it. They say he went to Oxford,' she said.

'Thought so. I can smell a wasted education from the top of the road.'

I unlocked the room and Shirley asked if she could use the bathroom. Always the first thing they do. I poured out two Scotches and took Sarah's picture from my pocket. I set it up again on the desk and looked out through the window at the London night. Brought back memories.

'Come on, Shirl, I'm sure you look beautiful.'

When she came out, she'd brushed her hair and relaxed. She was smiling.

'Money first, Harry, you know the rules.'

I put the fifty on the table. Shirley was sipping at her Scotch with a come-on smile that made her look younger. She was leaning back against the table and had crossed her legs. She always did have good legs. Long and thin with black stockings. She saw me looking at them, and rubbed one leg gently against the other.

'You sure, Harry, now that I'm here? I mean, I know how lonely you boys can get these long summer evenings. All alone on your stake-outs.'

'No, Shirley. But I know where to come if I should change my mind. Ever seen her?' I said, pointing to the photograph. Shirley picked it up and looked at it in a dreamy sort of way.

'May have done,' she said. 'There's a lot of girls out there, you know. I think it's the recession.'

'Shirley, this girl was murdered last night, her body dumped on your patch.'

'Oh she's the one, is she?'

'You've heard about it then?'

'Well, of course I've heard about it, Harry. When people start dumping dead bodies on the streets we work, we do usually get to hear about it.

'Something strange happened. Over the last few weeks. These girls came out. Completely fresh, not dressed right for this game, nobody knew them. Didn't fit, no one could connect with them at all. All went off with a punter just once, and all seemed to get picked up by the same one. Came in his car. The other girls said it was as though they were expecting him. Each one went off with him and was never seen again. Now with this one turning up dead, it's gone very quiet out there. Hush-hush. A lot of listening going on.'

The phone rang. It was nearly midnight.

'Just a minute, Shirley,' I said.

'Mind if I get some ice from Einstein downstairs? Never could drink this stuff without ice.'

'Come straight back then,' I said. 'I need a description of this punter and his car.'

Shirley went off to get her ice and I plugged in to Commissioner Tinley.

'Any progress, Selbourne?'

'Yes, I'm feeling my way into it, sir, but it's far too early for me to report anything as yet.'

'I'd like you to confide in me anything you consider germane to the case. Is that understood?'

'You have my word, Commissioner. Now I must get back to work, sir. I'm interviewing.'

'In your hotel? At midnight?'

'I have my own ways. That's why I've been brought in.'

'Evidently.' He put the phone down. I had to let some of

the whisky out. My bladder's not what it used to be, but then nothing else is either. There in the bathroom were the little flicks of blood against the inside of the basin and the used syringe in the wastebasket. So Shirley had shot up. That's why she'd seemed so breezy when she came out. And where, oh where, was she now?

I ran down to the bottom of the steps. He was there, but she wasn't.

'Where is she?' I shouted at him.

'What, your youthful companion?' he said, not looking up from his reading. 'She seemed under the impression that she'd served the police quite enough for one night. Gone off to find a sailor now, for a bit of variety in the uniform department, I shouldn't wonder.'

As I say, I'm out of condition and overweight, but a certain amount of basic training never leaves you, and I was over the other side of the counter before he knew what was happening. My face was only inches from his as he stumbled backwards, and I should think the smell of my whisky breath wasn't too pleasant as I hissed at him, 'Well, you go and bring the youthful lady back, Mr Ashburton, or you can start putting up the For Sale notices outside.'

By the time I turned away, he was scared and I was out of breath.

'Just do it,' I said. 'And don't come back till you've found her. I'll play hotel-keep for the rest of the night. Always wanted a steady job.'

An hour later he came back. Alone.

'She's not out there,' he said. 'Nobody is now. Lovely night for a walk, though. I suppose I should thank you for encouraging me to take more exercise.'

I went back up to the room, cursing myself for an idiot. Then I noticed for the first time that the fifty pounds on the table had gone.

2

The second day of the investigation.

Well, Sarah, what do you make of me, eh? Smiling so serenely out of your photograph on the table here, with your blonde hair and green eyes and your red bandanna wrapped high up over your head. Five foot five. Twenty-five. Beautiful. And dead. What do you make of the mastermind brought in here to find out what became of you, my love? So far I've brought a prostitute back here to shoot some smack, leave her bloody (and probably HIV-infected) needle in my basket, then go without giving me a description of the man you went off with on that final journey. You and the others. Who was he, Sarah? Are you going to help me? I look down at your words again:

Look at what is before you. Nothing is accidental. His name completes the saeculum. He must die last.

Now what did you mean by that, I wonder? Hardly an easy

clue, is it? Though I suppose I should be grateful you're not underestimating my intelligence. And who is 'he'? I phone up Frank, whose boys had been door-to-dooring.

'Anything?'

'She seems to be clean as a whistle. Real Sunday School material. No booze, no drugs, no men.'

'No women?'

'No. Didn't have her finger in any dyke that we can see. Sorry to disappoint you.'

'This thesis she was doing . . .'

'Yes, at the Quentin over at Roehampton. I spoke to her supervisor this morning. A Mr Adam Seed, B. Phil. He's deeply shocked, or at least he says he is. I said you might well want to see him today. He's teaching from ten to twelve. Otherwise any time at all. An amenable customer.'

'Can I have a squad car?'

'Use a cab, Harry, I'm booked.'

'I thought this was the top-priority case.'

'That was yesterday, my friend. Now's she's just another stiff with an impatient daddy. And make sure you keep all your receipts, won't you, Harry, or Accounts will give you hell, mate.'

'This Adam Seed. Any previous?'

'No, clean as the untrodden, just like Snow White.'

'Any Paddington connection?'

'Not that shows up here, anyway. Lives in Roehampton in a college flat.'

'Pathology established the hour of the injection yet?'

'Eight p.m. Give or take half an hour.'

'And our Mr Seed, B. Phil . . .'

'Has a cast-iron alibi. He was at a late meeting in college with Dr Antonia Sotheby. She's corroborated.'

'So he's out of it then?'

'Completely.'

'How long do Pathology say elapsed between death and dumping?'

'From the surface bruising, not long, not long at all, in fact. Maybe ten minutes.'

'Then it couldn't have been in her flat, could it Frank? You couldn't have got from Nevern Square to Leinster Gardens with a body, not with all those steps to go down as well, in ten minutes.'

'You could if you were speeding, officer.' I could hear him tapping away on his computer. He wasn't paying attention any more.

'But that's illegal, isn't it?' I said.

'Oh well,' he said distractedly, 'out of the question then, obviously.'

I had a walk around the streets in daylight. The girls would be asleep now, assuming they were all still alive. I kept circling Leinster Gardens, where she'd been dumped. Somebody here saw something, that was for sure. Whether they'd talk, though, was another question. There was so much dealing and shooting up and pimping here now that if people heard a scream on the street, they'd turn up the television and pull the curtains. Where was it you had that first big fix (for my instincts had decided it *was* her first) and why? Why didn't you struggle, my Sunday School mistress? Why did you take the end of your life so calmly?

The third cab agreed to take me to Roehampton after I pulled rank and showed him my badge.

'It's a long way, guv.'

'That's why I'm not planning on walking.'

'I'll never get a fare back again from there. Not these days, I won't.'

'Look,' I said, 'I'm a copper and I'm paid to chase villains, and you're a cabbie and you're paid to take fares. So take a fare, why don't you, and stop whining about it.'

'I'd say we do a bit better taking the fares than you do pulling the villains,' he said, as he turned into the traffic. 'Look at this in the paper: Police Commissioner's daughter murdered. If he can't even look after his own, what chance do the rest of us have?'

He had a point, though I didn't say so. I took the paper from him. Prostitution. Hard drugs overdose. The secret vice life of a perfect girl. The tabloid saints were in their pulpits already. I stuck the paper back through into the front of the cab.

'Don't believe everything you read in there,' I said.

'I don't believe anything I read in there.'

'Why'd you buy it then?'

'To wipe my arse on.'

I'd missed them, these intellectual chats with cab drivers. I couldn't remember having any Socratic discourses like this in the West Riding. When we got to the college, I paid him and he said, 'How long you going to be, then?'

'About twenty minutes, maybe half an hour.'

'And then you're going back to Craven Hill, are you?'

'No. Nevern Square, off Earls Court,' I said.

'I'll have a coffee and a sandwich over in that union bar and wait for you,' he said. 'If you come back and I'm not here, give a blip on the horn. I'll leave the door open.'

It seemed that I'd made a new friend after all.

Mr Seed: small, thin, ginger-haired and balding with a pair of wire-rimmed spectacles. About forty. Never seen anyone look less like a killer since I took the wife to see Vera Lynn at the Dominion. We sat down on either side of a small desk in his book-crammed study.

'Any ideas, Mr Seed?'

'About the death, you mean?'

'The killing, yes.'

'None, I'm afraid. A sign for the times.'

'Did Sarah have any kind of involvement that you knew of with drugs, prostitution, or with anyone connected in any way with either of those things?'

'Absolutely not. An exemplary student. Eccentric but exemplary.'

'In what way eccentric?'

'Her work, I mean, was ... unusual. Unorthodox. I

admired it greatly for its vigour and honesty. But there were some in the department who felt differently.'

'What *was* her thesis exactly?'

'Christian Figurings in Nineteenth-century English and American Literature.'

'You couldn't give me any kind of a notion . . .?'

'Are you acquainted at all with the last few decades of literary study and theory?'

'No. I know what I like, of course, same as the next man.'

Mr Seed's eyes flickered on and off me. It's curious how many intellectuals won't look you in the eye. I suppose it's the soul or nothing for those boys.

'There was a very popular type of literary theory not so many years ago which asserted the unimportance of the author, asserted that the author was, if you like, a mere conduit of language, a cypher almost of psychological and social structures. That the text wrote itself and used what we had traditionally called the author as its pen. Sarah started from this and added to it the claim by Borges that there was only one book, that all books were one book, that each writer simply added a few words or pages to the great book of the world. To this, Sarah then brought her rigorous teleological notion of time, and her commitment to Christian typology. This is how she read nineteenth-century English literature, finding in it patterns of Christian figurings even where none had ever been intended by the authors.'

'Did you approve of this work?' I asked, extremely unsure what that work was.

'I found it . . . exhilarating, I suppose,' he said. He looked at the far wall, a little uncomfortably I thought. Not like a man found guilty, though, more like a man in love. Despite my years away in the hills, my urban detective's instincts were coming back into play.

'Mr Seed, this is a very serious murder investigation and I must ask you to think carefully before answering the next question. Remember, a certain amount of embarrassment now might be better than arraignment for perverting the course of justice later. Were you having an affair with Sarah Tinley?'

For the first time he relaxed, threw back his head and laughed with authentic merriment.

'With Sarah? No, that would have been quite impossible. Nobody . . . not with Sarah . . .'

I still carried on. I'd seen something in him.

'You were in love with her though, weren't you?' He stopped laughing and behind those thick convex specs of his there was something glistening, though I wasn't sure what.

'Yes,' he said, 'yes, I was. We all were, if you must know. You won't find anyone who knew her who wasn't.'

'Excepting the one, presumably?'

'I don't know,' he said. 'I wouldn't know that. How could anybody know that? Until you solve the puzzle, that is.'

My cab driver took me back over to Nevern Square. His bacon sandwich had upped his sugar level and he'd picked up the energy needed to tell me about his wife, his twin boys,

his daughter (who was heading for disaster), his mortgage
and, as we swung into Earls Court, the strange pains that had
started up in his scrotum over the last few weeks. I was glad
to get out. As he jingled my change, I said, 'Could somebody
get from here to Leinster Gardens at eight o'clock on a
Friday evening in less than ten minutes?'

'No,' he said, 'well, not unless he was using a police
helicopter.' It was only as he turned the corner that I
registered I'd not asked for a receipt. Fifty quid's worth of
taxi rides. Accounts. Now I'd have to fiddle some expenses,
as if I didn't have enough problems.

Back in Sarah's flat I poured myself some of her whisky
and sat at her desk. She must have liked to look down on the
world while she worked, the same as I did. I started making
my way through her bookshelves. She certainly did have a
lot of things on nineteenth-century literature, English and
American. And on millennial expectations. And on Christianity and apocalypse. As her supervisor had said, she was
obviously an exemplary student. Then I found one tatty little
magazine tucked in behind the books, *Millennium Bulletin*.
This one I knew, this one I often flicked through myself,
since it had the names of many of the main groups waiting
for the end of the world to come and enthrone them in
glory. It might have been of a purely technical interest to her,
how could I know? Anyway it was something, so I slipped it
in my bag, along with another five copies of her black
notebooks. I washed up the glass and left. It was a sunny day

and so I walked back up to Craven Hill. Inside the hotel, little boy blue was listening to the radio.

'Any calls?' I said.

'Yeah, King Charles wants you to join him for polo this afternoon, then become his intelligence agent.'

'Watch it, son,' I said. 'Just watch it, remember.'

Up in the room I had a bath and tried a little meditative thought. None of this was fitting together, none of it. Sarah was Snow White one day, and the next her veins were full of heroin, she was naked and dead except for an embroidered white smock, and was now being accused of soliciting in Paddington. The only lead I had was the man Shirley had seen, and I'd let Shirley go without getting a description of the john or his car. I was a disgrace to the force. The phone rang before I was dry. You can probably guess who.

'Any developments, Detective-Sergeant?'

'Nothing specific, Commissioner. I'm still collating, of course.'

'You will let me know?'

'I will indeed.'

He didn't sound that concerned to me, all of a sudden. Maybe he wanted it all to die, just like she had. A story in the papers today, forgotten tomorrow. Maybe he hoped it would all quietly disappear. It wouldn't, though, not as long as I had any say in the matter.

I sat at the table by the window and looked through *Millennium Bulletin*. Lots of stuff about the return of Merlin, the inauguration of the New Age, apocalypse and the latest serial killings in Berlin. Most of this was off the wall. You'd have to be a real devotee. I found it hard to believe that Sarah could have been. Surely she was too bright to be reading this junk? On the classified ads page at the back, she had ringed an entry:

> *The Patmos Group. Little flock tomorrow. Paddington. The left hand should not know what the right is doing.*

I looked at the date of the *Bulletin*. The second. She had died on the third. I was on the phone to Frank straight away.

'Frank, can you key in *Millennium Bulletin* and find out if there's anyone of ours can tell me about it?'

I heard the tap-tapping of his keyboard.

'Yes, indeed there is,' he said. 'Fellow called Harry Selbourne. Want his address, do you, up in the West Riding?'

I put the phone down. I called the number given on the bottom of the sheet. It was an answering device for placing classifieds. I checked the address. Shepherd's Bush.

When I arrived there, it turned out to be one room in a half-derelict 1930s block. No answer to my banging. An old lady from the next flat peered round her chained door very cautiously. I held up my badge to her from a distance.

'Police,' I said. 'Detective-Sergeant Selbourne, CID Research and Appraisal. Who lives here, do you know?'

'Nobody lives there,' she said. 'A man and a woman use it

in the evenings. They run some sort of news-sheet. An end-of-the-world calendar or something.'

'What are they like?'

'Pleasant enough. They take drugs, I should think, if that's what you're after, but then they all do round here, love. They've always been nice enough to me. Called an ambulance for me once.'

'When do they usually turn up?'

'Evening,' she said. 'Sometimes late evening. Sometimes not at all.'

I went down to the end of the corridor and took out my mobile. I phoned Frank.

'I need a warrant Frank and a screwdriver man down here pronto. I may be on to something.'

'I'll have to check,' he said.

'Then check and phone back.'

I stood there counting the cobwebs for ten minutes. Finally the phone rang.

'Sorry, Harry, nothing doing.'

'This could be of importance in the Tinley killing. Would you prefer it if I went over your head straight to the Commissioner?'

'The very gentleman I've just finished speaking to, as a matter of fact. Wants everything done by the book, Harry. Application in writing for the warrant. In triplicate, if I remember rightly.'

'What's going on, Frank?'

'Search me. Maybe the interest's shifting. Three people

jumped simultaneously from the National Westminster building this morning. Not one of them over twenty. A nation mourns, you know, but it has something new to mourn with every day that passes.'

He put the phone down on me. I stood wondering what to do. There was a whispering sound up the corridor. The old lady had her hand out through the crack in the door. She was holding some keys. I walked up there.

'I keep these for them, but you can't be too careful,' she said. She must have been eighty-five, even ninety, an ancient dusty face the world had left to its own devices here. I took the keys, walked down the corridor, and let myself into the flat. A chaos of books, papers, old copies of the *Bulletin*. A few dead tabs in ashtrays. They were dope heads, no hard stuff, I could tell just by breathing. This was E.T. territory, cosmic vibrations, holistic cures. This wasn't murder and needles, I knew. I locked up again and pinned a note to the door: *Please Contact me ASAP on this Number. Urgently. D.S.Selbourne.*

I left and found the nearest pub, where I ordered a double. So, it was a non co-op. My fellow cops just weren't co-opping. They didn't want to know. It could have been any number of things. Maybe the Commissioner and his wife felt the worst was over and that was it. Any more details would be salt in the wound. One more random killing in the big bad city. Maybe the Met boys had done for me. I could just hear them: 'He's over the hill, been up in the sticks for nearly ten years, couldn't get his fingers round the collar of a kebab these days. Fat and wheezy. Should never have been brought in. Send him back home to his Noddy books and the mystical claptrap on his computer.'

Maybe they were right, too. I went back to the hotel and started trying to read through Sarah's notebooks. At six I went out and found a curry house. I took one of her notebooks with me. It was fascinating, I found it all fascinating, but it wasn't getting me any closer to anything.

I arrived back at the hotel around nine. Our boy informed me there was a message. A Mr Dick England of the *Millennium Bulletin* had called. I phoned him back. The voice on the other end was sleepy, drawly, a dope head, as I'd suspected.

'You ran an ad on the second,' I said. 'Patmos Group. Ring any bells?'

'Classified?'

'Yes.'

'Don't even bother listening to them. Pass the tape straight over to the printer. They input direct up there.'

'When's the next issue?'

'Be on the streets tomorrow evening.'

'How do I get a copy?'

'Thompson's on the Earls Court Road takes it.'

'Thanks, then,' I said, and put the phone down. That night I went out on to the streets again. No Shirley, and no one else I knew who could do a positive ID. So I went back to the hotel and finished the bottle of whisky.

Next morning the phone was ringing before I was up. It was the Commissioner.

'Anything?'

'No sir,' I said. 'Doesn't seem to be much in the way of co-operation either.'

'Everything must be done according to procedure. Did the warrant turn out to be necessary after all?'

'No sir, it didn't,' I said.

'There we are then.' He hung up.

I phoned Frank. He sounded weary, uninterested, too preoccupied with the tap-tap-tapping of his keyboard.

'Couldn't spare me the time for a pint this lunchtime, could you?'

I could hear him thinking about it.

'How long do we go back, Frank? Twenty-five years?'

'All right,' he said. 'You remember the Rose and Crown?'

'Off the Embankment?'

'One o'clock. I've got twenty-five minutes maximum, Harry.'

'One for every year of our liaison, then. How time does fly.'

I was there before him, sipping away at a pint. When he came in I waved him over.

'You'll have a pint, Frank?'

'Mineral water. Drink on your breath at the station these days, you get sent home.' I *had* been away a long time.

I looked at him as he sipped his sparkling water. Thin,

intense, balding, high forehead, sharp brown eyes. He was a good officer, but the joy had all drained out of him.

'So what's the word then?'

He lit a cigarette. At least he'd kept one vice. 'You want it straight?'

'Don't think we've got time for anything kinky have we?'

He didn't smile. My jokes belonged back on the moors, with the sheep and fog.

'The word's this, Harry: you should never have been brought down. You're out of shape and out of time. Been away from these streets too long to be any use on them. You're an archive man, never be anything else now.

'Except the Commissioner had a little flurry of excitement at the beginning. Wanted the expert on all this apocalypse crap. Somebody bangs a computer keyboard. *MK* they key in, and your name gets spewed out. Then two things happen. First you turn up here looking like an out-of-work librarian, and impressing nobody at all, then someone talks stats to the Commissioner.'

'Stats, Frank?'

'It's all stats now, Harry. There's nothing but stats any more. We classify the crime then feed it into the stats programme. That tells us the solve rate in that area, and on that basis we calculate how much police time should be invested.'

'And the stats on this?'

'About as bad as they come, my friend. Last year in London we had maybe ten thousand OD deaths. Who knows how many were self-administered, and how many received a helping hand from a loved one? The clean-up rate's about one per cent. We now reckon it's the most popular form of murder because we never can be sure whether it is murder anyway. Even if they get caught, they plead euthanasia. Throw in your end-of-the-world caper and it gets even murkier. We don't even touch WW – it's not worth it unless they kill a politician.'

'WW?' I asked innocently.

'Warlocks and wankers, Harry. You see, you've been away too long. Don't even know the terminology, sitting up there in Yorkshire reading your science fiction.

'And someone who shall remain nameless had a little word in the Commissioner's ear, pointing out that given all these unsolved crimes and all these grieving parents, it might perhaps look a little odd if suddenly within days his own little girl gets her case solved. Word is our Commissioner will be Minister for Culture next year. Not that he's got all that much culture himself, mind you, but his wife's dripping with the stuff, and would much prefer to be going to the royal box in Covent Garden than being polite to the smelly brigade out on the streets, and technically speaking, that's still you and me, even though neither of us ever go near a street any more. So it would be a shame if the press suddenly got hold of the idea that our lord and master had been pulling any strings.'

'What about me then, Frank?'

'You've got a week here on expenses, then they're

shipping you home. If I were you, I'd forget all about your virgin hooker, and take in a few shows instead. You won't be getting invited to London any more, I'll promise you that much.'

'Thanks for filling me in, then.'

'My pleasure. Don't make waves. No more calls for warrants, all right? Check out the second-hand bookshops, Harry. Enjoy yourself at the expense of the Met. Now I've got to go. I'm running a big programme. Take care of yourself, old son.'

'And you.'

Frank left. So now I knew. They've abandoned you to your death, Sarah. You're not worth pursuing. I went back to Nevern Square. I still had the key to her flat in my pocket.

3

That night I drank Sarah's whisky. I read Sarah's books and I slept in Sarah's sheets. I put her photograph next to me on the bedside table. This was the consummation of our marriage. One of us dead and the other alive, but only just. In the morning I tidied the place up, locked it and went down the steps. Next to the door there was a pile of mail. On the top was a shrink-wrapped envelope addressed to Sarah Tinley. I slipped it into my bag and meandered out to find the nearest café. I could only face coffee. I sat staring out into the Earls Court Road. I opened up the packet. It was

the *Millennium Bulletin*. Of course, she had been a subscriber.
I flipped through it. The usual insanities about messages from
Phaeton and talking microbes. When I got to the Classified
Ads I scanned down blearily. There it was:

The Patmos Group. Paddington. Tomorrow.
Instruments of the Passion. The second nail.

I bit the cup. I opened the bag for the mobile, but I'd left it
at the hotel. I'd been incommunicado. I lurched down to the
counter of the café. The man there was breaking eggs into a
huge frying pan.

'Phone,' I said. 'I need a phone.'

'Can't use this one,' he said. 'Down the bottom of the
street there . . .'

But I was already round the other side of the counter,
picking up the receiver and waving my badge at him.

'Police,' I muttered. 'Emergency. Frank, I . . .'

'And where exactly have you been? Do you know what
we've got on our hands?'

'Surprise me,' I said. 'Number two?'

'At the morgue, in twenty minutes.'

The man driving the taxi wanted to talk to me. I didn't
want to talk to him, though, and I told him so. I kept staring
at that classified ad in the *Bulletin*. I could have bought it last
night at the newsagent's. But I'd already switched off by
then. Exactly like Frank had told me to. I had a funny feeling
he might have forgotten all about our conversation.

It was D11 again. About thirty. Dark hair, small, very slight. No particular distinguishing marks, except for the one: an omega on her left palm. Four inches above it the needle had gone in and delivered five grammes of pure heroin. A white shift again. The same reference to Revelation. This time above it the letter N.

'Where did they find her, Frank?'

'Threadneedle Street. By the portico of the Bank.'

'Time?'

'About nine p.m.'

'Am I to take it that your previous remarks about the conduct of this case are now inoperative?'

'Get back on to it, Harry. And find something, will you? Fucking pronto, amigo. They're worried about the press more than anything else. Nobody gives a tinker's fart about the stiffs, but they don't like it when these cat and mousers start up. It makes us look like a bunch of jerks, and it starts to make the great British public nervous. Oh, and one other thing. Make no contact with the Commissioner. Under any circumstances whatsoever.'

'Not even if my investigation requires it?'

'Make sure your investigation does not require it, that's all. You still staying at the Zorba?'

'Yes.'

'Each to his own. We've opened an account for you at the NatWest up the road there. Here's the chequebook. A thousand a week maximum till further notice. Keep the receipts.'

Back at the hotel, I pinned a large map of London to the wall, as the Met's grapevine sparkie installed the fax. Two red pinheads on either side of the city. I had a taste in my mouth that hadn't been so bad since the day my wife walked out with my son. I also had an uncanny feeling all this was going to get a lot worse. But then they do say it's always darkest before the dawn.

An identical manner of death. When the pathologist's report came in, it established about forty-five minutes between the death and the depositing of the body, judging by the bruising when it hit the pavement. Just long enough to get from Paddington over to Threadneedle Street. I was camped in the right place all right, I was sure of that. But what was the point? Who was doing what to whom and why? One death on the third, another on the sixth.

I spent the rest of the day in the hotel, reading Sarah's notebooks. Every so often a line would be asterisked. I made a list of some of these:

Chastisement, repentance, glory

nunc est tempus propriam Antichristi

Radix peccati – the root of sin is in the human body

Let the cross prevail over the Whore of Babylon

After reading all this, I felt I needed another talk with Mr Seed. I also began to wonder if I might possibly have been taken in by his dithery intellectual manner. I decided he had more to tell me than I'd heard so far, and I also wanted to know where he had been the evening before.

'Paris, addressing a conference.'

'You're sure, Frank?'

'I'm sure. I've checked. Forget him.'

'All the same, I want to see him as soon as he's back. Do we have a positive yet, on the new one?'

'Yes, she's Patricia Carleon of Notting Hill. Thirty years old. One-time schoolteacher. Of late, a shop assistant at the Notting Hill Community Trust.'

'Anything else?'

'Not much.'

That afternoon I called in at the Community Trust. A nice old lady, grey-haired and stooped in her fluffy cardigan, stood behind the counter beaming at everyone in the shop.

'I'm sorry to trouble you,' I said, 'but do you know Patricia Carleon?'

'Yes,' she said. 'In fact, she should be here today. I'm afraid I don't know where she is though.'

'I do,' I said. 'Could we go round the back there and talk for a minute?' I showed her my badge. We went into a room filled with old clothes and shoes.

'Patricia is dead, I'm afraid,' I said. 'Murdered, we suspect. I'm trying to find out something that can help us find out what happened. Is there anything you can think of which might possibly be of help?'

'Patricia murdered?' she said. 'Why, the poor girl. The

poor poor girl. And she was so . . . quiet. A nice girl, I suppose, strange in her way, but nice.'

A large lady suddenly joined us, holding aloft a lace dress.

'They've been putting the size fourteens on to the twelve hangers again, you know. It's really no wonder they fall off, is it? I mean, is it?' She left then, gravely shaking her head.

'In what way strange?' I said. The old lady was still shaking her own head in disbelief.

'What?' she said.

'You said Patricia was strange. In what way?'

'Well, it was these funny religious beliefs she had, that she used to go on and on about. We finally had to ask her to stop, you know. Some of the customers complained, they found it all a bit . . . unsettling.'

'What beliefs, Mrs . . .'

'Dickinson. And its Miss actually. They called themselves Magdalenas, the little Magdalenas, the women who sold themselves for Jesus.'

'You mean Patricia was a prostitute?'

'Well, I wouldn't have put it like that. Not exactly, anyway. Well, only once, I think, if I remember what she said correctly. It was all very odd. You only had to do it once. Then you qualified.'

'Qualified for what?'

'Something about sinking to the bottom. No one could be raised who'd not descended.'

'To sin in order to be redeemed?'

'Something very like that, yes. Reminded me of Rasputin,

that was pretty much his line, if I recall. I heard all about it when I was a girl. Anyway I said, "My dear child, even if I wanted to, which I most certainly do not, at my age it would be quite out of the question." '

'Was there a man connected with this?'

'Well, I suppose there must have been, mustn't there? Always is. But she never spoke of it again, not after that one time. Not a word, once she'd seen that I wasn't really very keen. She was very polite, you see. Kept herself very much to herself. Yet, you know the odd thing was, apart from that one attempt to make me into a Magdalena, I'd have said she was more like a Sunday School teacher than anything else.'

'Another one,' I said to myself.

'Sorry?'

'Never mind. If you think of anything else that might help, please call this number, would you? You've really been very helpful.'

I walked back up through the small streets that link Notting Hill and Paddington. It sounded like the oldest story in the book. Give me your body and I'll give you revelation and redemption. Free the spirit from the flesh that still imprisons it. Could Sarah really have fallen for that one? And who was the Svengali, Rasputin, Jim Jones, David Koresh? The only person I knew who could give me an ID was Shirley.

When I arrived back at the hotel I phoned Frank and told him we had to find Shirley. Shirley Hensher – well at least that was what she'd been called the last time I'd asked for her full particulars, which was some years back. Frank was not impressed.

'This your best lead then, is it, Harry?'

'As things stand, yes.'

'All right, I'll tell every member of the force out there to look for a ginger-haired tom and user, mid-forties, no fixed abode, travelled under the name of Shirley Hensher fifteen years ago. But you won't be holding your breath, will you?'

I could see what he meant.

'When's Seed back?'

'Saturday morning. But why keep on about him?'

'He understands something about what Sarah Tinley believed, and that could be the key to all this. There's something about him. I don't know.'

I phoned the number in Paris and arranged to meet him when he landed at Heathrow.

That Saturday was the eighth. The next edition of *Millennium Bulletin* was already out. There was no reference to the Patmos Group, but one entry bothered me. It read:

> *By which you may know, wherever you go,*
> *The warranted genuine Snarks.*

In the notebooks there were references to Lewis Carroll. But then there were references to almost everyone else too. When I met Seed, I showed him the ad.

'Mean anything?'

'Someone quoting Lewis Carroll, *The Hunting of the Snark*. What can I say?'

'You don't think it might be relevant to this investigation?' We were walking down towards the taxis. I'd said I'd drop him off, to give us time to talk.

'I don't actually know what this investigation is, as a matter of fact, do you? All right, listen. *The Hunting of the Snark* was one of Sarah's texts, but there were plenty of others, don't forget. When Dodgson wrote it, it's thought he might have been trying to lift the spirits of his godson, Charlie Wilcox. Charlie was suffering from what the Victorians called an inflammation of the lungs, and what we'd now call tuberculosis. Anyway, Dodgson nursed him, and one day he took a walk over the Surrey Downs to get away from it all and, so he tells us, a line came to him out of nowhere – "*For the Snark was a Boojum, you see*" – the last line of the poem. He started at the end and worked backwards. It's a poem of reversal. It's literally preposterous, back to front. The ship in the poem goes in reverse. And Sarah saw many things in it, as she saw many things in every text she ever dealt with. She believed that Henry Holiday's illustrations alluded to Breughel's *The Ship of Fools* in the Louvre. There are twelve figures in Breughel's boat, and Sarah was convinced they represented a parodic inversion of the twelve apostles. In the poem, whatever the Bellman says three times is true: so there's the Trinity. There seem to be allusions to Christ's stigmata, and the one who immolates himself to discover the snark at the end is a baker. He made bread, just as Jesus did miraculously to feed the five thousand, just as he broke it before and after he died.' He stopped then, as though exhausted by these inexhaustible interpretations.

'Did it cheer up Charlie Wilcox, then?' I asked.

'He died before he ever got to hear a word of it.'

'Know anything about the Magdalenas, Mr Seed?' There was something there, I could sense it.

'Sarah spoke sometimes . . .'

'Come on, man, there are two people dead already.'

'It was part of Sarah's scheme. I told you she had eccentric ideas. Christ lowered himself down to the depths, consorted with the wretched of the earth, got tortured to death as a common criminal. She thought the feminists made a terrible mistake wanting to be priests. They should lower themselves down too, become whores and then . . .'

'And then what?'

'Die,' he said, turning and looking at me straight for the first time. 'Help ruin the great work of time. Hurry the end along. The sooner the better, in her view.'

'You don't know any of these other Magdalenas?'

'No.'

'Or the man they did their sinking to the depths with?'

'No.'

'I'd say he'd got one of the better jobs this century, wouldn't you?'

We had reached the college gates at Roehampton.

'You have my number here,' he said. 'Call if there's anything I can do to help, though I can't see how.' This was

49

real grief too. A lot of people had a hole in their hearts where Sarah Tinley had disappeared.

I told the driver to stop at Westone's bookshop by the station, where I bought *The Hunting of the Snark*. In Part Two I found the quote:

> *Come, listen, my men, while I tell you again*
> *The five unmistakable marks*
> *By which you may know, wheresoever you go,*
> *The warranted genuine Snarks.*

The next morning my phone rang at six a.m.

'Another two bodies have been found, sir. You'd best come to the morgue.'

By the time I arrived Frank was there too.

'No tattoos this time.'

'You sure?'

'They've had quite a good look. Haven't seen anything.'

'Sir,' called out one of the attendants. 'Sorry, sir, I've just found them.'

He pulled back the sheets to reveal one omega tattooed on the left sole of the first body and the second on the right sole of the other. It turned out the injections had been made a few inches higher in each ankle.

'Where were they found?' I said.

'Thessaly Road. Just below New Covent Garden.'

They wore the same white shifts, but with two different letters embroidered on them – one an R and one an I.

I went back to the hotel and did what I should have done at the beginning: I had the incoming calls to the *Bulletin* offices taped. We'd had one death on the 3rd, one on the 6th and now two on the 9th. It seemed logical to expect the next one (or three) on the 12th.

For two days I read the notebooks, read them with whisky and read them without it. There was too much in them. Almost any line could be a key. Here was a page:

Out of bondage. Egypt. Baudelaire's hell was Hell. The experience that had decayed was the experience of redemption. The millenarian comfort: that time can shuffle off at last into justice. Harlequin parades of revolution, paradise conquered by force and instituted here on the earth's mottled skin. From Blake: the marriage of heaven and earth, the end of the earth. A coitus between the light and dark. Once the mind is fixed on eschatology, everyone around is simply an ending waiting to happen. Spiritual euthanasia – to be delivered from this world into the hands of the Lord. Donatello: Magdalena so ravaged there's only divine love left for her to solicit. When Wilde wrote his ballad in Reading Gaol he was known as Prisoner C.3.3. The third letter of the alphabet and the trinitarian number. De Profundis. Nothing is ever accidental. A to Z. Auschwitz. The saeculum is in its final stage. Zennor.

The phone rang. It was Frank.

'One of these girls lived in a flat off Westbourne Grove. Judy Flint. Was known to frequent the Catholic church around the corner there, St Michael and All Angels. Perhaps you'd care to have a chat with the padre, one Father Praed.'

By the time I got down there it was late afternoon. Four or five drunks and semi-drunks were sprawled along the stone corridor that led to the presbytery. They were all unexpectedly affable.

'If it's the Father you want, he's inside, go right ahead,' they said.

He was small and looked tired, his grey hair thin but still there on his head. He looked like someone nothing could surprise any more. He kept moving the rosary in his right hand.

'I can't get up, I'm afraid,' he said. 'This arthritis makes it worse than moving houses. Judy, yes,' he said quietly, 'I didn't know her well. Dead is she? God bless her. Such a young girl. She's with the Lord now, anyway.'

'She certainly thought so,' I said. 'Have you come across the Magdalenas, Father?'

He looked sad.

'Yes, I've heard about them. Lay down your body and your pride for Christ. Foolish girls. Christ never wanted that of anyone. He bid them cease. Was Judy . . .?'

'We think so. That seems to be the pattern. Did you ever notice if Judy was accompanied by a man at all?'

'No, she seemed if anything like a . . .'

'Sunday School teacher?'

'I was going to say a nun actually, but suit yourself.'

There was a knock on the door. A man swayed in. His face was swollen, one eye black. He was in bad shape. I made a note to myself to cut down on the whisky.

'I'll leave then,' I said leaning across and shaking the old priest's hand. He made the sign of the cross over me, but he was already looking sadly at his new visitor.

'You've been on the drink again then, Sammy?'

No message came in to the *Bulletin* on the 11th and no bodies were found on the 12th, or the 13th. And I couldn't stand one more day in the Zorba. I told Frank I was going on the train down to Brighton just for the night. I gave him the hotel address, packed up my laptop and a change of clothes and left.

I had forgotten how sordid Brighton is these days, but at least the sea is there. I can always think more clearly by the sea.

I bought myself a Scotch at a bar on the pier. From there I could look across at the other pier, the ruined one. The starlings would swoop like an intelligent cloud and disappear inside the rotting rafters and the crooked iron. I knew that all the information needed was as surely packed inside my head as the starlings were in the wreck of that pier, but I simply couldn't find the shape of it all. It was like a story being told backwards, but I couldn't get to the starting point.

I walked down along the front until I found an empty seat. There was not a single sign of violence on any of these dead people. The syringe had slipped in sweetly each time. If these had been forced injections, there'd have been some puncturing of the surrounding skin: it would have been inevitable. From the first, I'd thought Sarah was no murder victim.

There was a pattern to it all, though – I was sure of that. Only I was too stupid to see it.

I walked down near the Pavilion. There's a little chapel there and I went in (I don't know why) and sat in the front pew. I looked up at the cross. Well, I thought, if you were ever planning on giving me any inspiration, Lord, now wouldn't be a bad time. I stared up at that crucifix for five, maybe even ten minutes. I saw the wounds painted red on the plaster. Then it started to sink in at last, the letters above his head. INRI. Sarah's embroidery showed an I, not a One as we'd thought, Patricia Carleon was N, Judy Flint and her friend of the twelfth were R and I. *Iesus Nazarenus Rex Iudaeorum*. Jesus Christ, King of the Jews. I walked back quickly to the hotel on the seafront where I'd booked for the night. I took out the *A to Z*. I plotted the four bodies. Sure enough they formed a cross. The five unmistakable signs, Christ's stigmata. One on both hands, one on both feet, and that meant there was still one to go: on the side. My mind was moving at last. I wrote the dates down: 3rd, 6th, 9th and – I'd assumed an additive progression, and was nonplussed when nothing happened on the 12th. It was too easy and I'd been getting lazy. As fat in my mind as I was in my body. It was an algorithm, a Fibonacci series. Add three to itself and get six, six to three gave you nine, the next one would be nine to six and that gave fifteen. Tomorrow.

What had she said? *Look at what is before you. Nothing is accidental. His name completes the saeculum. He must die last.* The phone rang. It was Frank.

'Your lucky day, Harry. I have here with me a Miss Shirley Hensher.'

'Put her on, Frank. I need to talk to her right now.'

Her voice came on the phone.

'I'm sorry, Harry, I suppose that wasn't very nice what I did the other night . . .'

'Never mind, Shirley. The man you saw, the one the girls all went with, what did he look like?'

'Nothing much. Small, thin, ginger hair. Wire-rimmed glasses.'

'Can you remember the car?'

'Yes, it was an old white Volkswagen.'

I turned back the page to one of the passages in her notebooks she had asterisked, a poem by Emily Dickinson:

> *Elijah's Wagon knew no thill*
> *Was innocent of Wheel*
> *Elijah's horses as unique*
> *As was his vehicle*

'There's one other thing, Harry,' Shirley said. 'There was a woman already in the car with him. That's what struck me as so odd.'

'What did she look like?'

'Mid-fifties. Dressed for a funeral. Very proper.'

'Put me back on to Frank, would you?'

Frank came on the line.

'Listen, you nail Seed this time.'

'Anthony Zennor Seed, you've got it.'

I felt an odd chill go through me.

'What did you just say, Frank?'

'Anthony Zennor Seed, that's the boy's full name. I have his file here in front of me.'

'Look at what is in front of you. Nothing is accidental. His name completes the saeculum. He must die last. A to Z.'

'What are you rambling on about, Harry?'

'Dr Antonia Sotheby, pull her in as well.'

'On what charge?'

'Make one up. Just pull them both in, Frank. Have you checked the tape from the *Bulletin* today?'

'Yes. Nothing. Just one line in a foreign language we could make neither head nor tail of. Otherwise nothing.'

'I want the foreign language one checked out, Frank.'

'We don't even know which language it's in. That can be expensive.'

'Then get your most expensive boffin on it. Another death could cost you more. I'll be with you in two hours.'

I threw my things into a bag and ran downstairs, flashed my badge at the receptionist and told her she'd be contacted later about the paying of my bill. Outside there was a cab. I got in and told him to take me to the station.

'Give it a break will you? I've been waiting here for half an hour. It's only five minutes walk up the road.'

I flashed the badge at him, too.

'Move it or I'll book you for obstructing the highway.'

I made the train with one minute to go. I still didn't entirely understand, but I'd begun at last to see a pattern, and it was the pattern that had been eluding me. I didn't believe Seed was a murderer, but I knew he was somehow connected with all this. As for Dr Sotheby, no one had even bothered to look. A nice touch for Seed to be in Paris while one of the dumpings took place. She was a small girl, that one. A woman could have lifted her out of the car.

When I arrived at Victoria, I got straight into a cab and was with Frank twenty minutes later.

'Seed, Dr Sotheby?'

'Not to be found today, either of them.'

'You checked the doctor out yet?'

'She rents a flat, 66 Westbourne Gardens, W2. Sorry, Harry, we were covering this side. We should have been a little more circumspect.'

'What about the tape?'

'Here comes the man himself.'

A tall thin character of about thirty was walking down the corridor towards us, holding a tape in one hand and a book in the other. He was looking pleased with himself.

'So which language are we talking about, sunshine?'

'Oh English,' the boffin said. 'English sure enough, but a thousand or so years back. It's Old English. It's from "The Dream of the Rood". Listen. This is what's on the tape: *uppe on þām eaxlegespanne.*'

He stared at us for a moment, daring one of us to know what it might mean. We didn't of course.

'Up on the crossbeam,' he said, smiling. 'It's about the cross of Christ you see and it says, "The corners of the earth/ Gleamed with fair jewels, just as there were five/ Upon the crossbeam."'

'You got a big map of London in there, Frank?'

'Through in Data Control,' he said.

Standing in front of it with a ruler and a pencil, I drew the lines and they intersected at Dean Street, Soho.

'That's where our next body will appear.'

'You seem very sure of yourself,' he said.

'It's where the crossbeam meets the upright,' I said. 'It's where the last of the five unmistakable signs has to end up. Have we means of access to Dr Sotheby's flat?'

'A master key acquired from the landlord. At least I got one thing right.' He handed it to me.

I suppose I arrived over at 66 Westbourne Gardens around six. There were seven golden candlesticks on the table. The tattooing gear was over in the corner. I touched it – still warm. Photographs of the five women were framed on a bookshelf and in the middle of them, Mr Anthony Zennor Seed. And every book about apocalypse ever written. I looked through some of them. Frank phoned.

'You want some protection, Harry?'

'Don't think so. He wouldn't hurt anybody. That's the bit that kept confusing me.'

At nine the phone rang.

'Your pencil might have needed sharpening. Only missed

it by an inch. It was Carlisle Street. Our Lady Antonia. Just found her. A white Volkswagen seen leaving the scene, but we lost him, I'm afraid.'

'It doesn't matter. You found her tattoo?'

'Yes, this one was a bit surprising . . .'

'Underneath her breast?'

'How did you know that?'

'Detective work, Frank, but never mind. I'll wait here for him. He'll be here soon enough.'

Twenty minutes later he came through the door. He didn't seem surprised to see me.

'That the lot then?' I said.

'You found Dr Sotheby?'

'We found her.'

'Then that's the lot. Except for me, of course.'

'He must die last.'

'In the bathroom there I have some . . . I don't suppose you'd consider being so kind as to administer for me . . .'

'Can't do it, Adam. Sorry. Career on the line. Pension. Everything.'

'I understand,' he said.

'Was it your idea?'

'God, no. I could never have dreamt up anything like this. To plan all this you'd have to have more vision than I ever did. Not a single one of them was hurt, you know – in any way. Everyone did what was agreed upon. And no suicides. We simply helped one another towards the end.'

'I'd already worked that out,' I said. 'No struggles, no

fights. I could see that.' I stood up and walked over to the drinks' table.

'A whisky?' I said.

'Prefer a brandy, if you don't mind.'

'Why, though?' I said as I sat back down.

'Her belief was so strong, the rest of us believed too.'

'Do you still believe now?'

'It was easier when she was in the room with me. But, yes, I believe. I have nothing else to believe. So why shouldn't I believe her? She shone with more light than anyone else I've ever known.'

'You were the man, weren't you?'

'The degrader, yes.'

'The one decent part of the job, I'd imagine?'

'No,' he said with a vehemence that startled me. 'That was the worst part of everything. I begged her to let me out of it. Do you know what it is to want someone that badly and then only be allowed once . . . and then the others too. I hated it. In any case it was only a ritual for her. It could have been anyone. It was easier to trust me with it, that's all.'

I looked at him over the rim of the glass.

'You really did love her didn't you, Adam?'

'Everybody did. When they talked about Christ, how people gave up their lives and followed him, it was like that with her.'

'You don't think . . . you don't think she could have been evil?'

'No,' he said, 'I don't. And I have a feeling you don't either. It's life without her that's the evil.'

'But Christ didn't ask people to commit suicide.'

'And neither did she. The little flock decided, and we administered unto one another. So that each of us could be a sign. The sign of the victorious cross laid across the Whore of Babylon, and made out of the whores themselves. The ultimate message to the world that hell itself is spelling out the name of heaven, that the realms are to be reconciled, that time is ending. It was our duty now to hurry it along. The law was dying so that love could prevail. But we were called upon to make a sacrifice. How many cities has the swastika laid its shadow over in the last hundred years. That crippled cross. We would turn it all round. The priest-king used to die to redeem the land. Now whores would lift us to heaven. They're not the beast – the beast is the one crushing them. The real Whore of Babylon is a man. The victims lie beneath him. Spread-eagled.

'How could she have anything but contempt for the law? Look at her father. What's his law? Greed. Hypocrisy. Pretence. How could she respect that? But that's this world. The only thing you could do with this world was to bring it to an end as soon as possible, not by killing others but by offering up yourself to show there's no cause to fear death. How many people stay alive only because they're too afraid to die?'

'Out of interest, Adam, before the boys turn up to take you in,' I said, 'Zennor?'

'My parents went there on honeymoon, and that's where I was conceived. For Sarah nothing was accidental, everything was written in time. That is what was so enchanting about it.'

The uniforms arrived a half hour later and Adam was taken away in cuffs, though I told them there was no need to bother. It looked better for the photographers, I suppose. The next day I received a call at the hotel from the Commissioner.

'I gather I should congratulate you on finding the killer.'

'Not quite sir,' I said. 'There was no killer. Your daughter went willingly to her death, as did all the others. If any one individual was a moving force in it, I'd have to say that it was almost certainly Sarah, not Adam Seed. She was the one with the vision.'

'Don't much like the sound of that, Selbourne, and I'd advise you not to go broadcasting any such opinion about the place.' He put the phone down.

I spent two days writing up the reports and had one night left in the smoke before I was due to head up north. I wandered out and had a Greek meal, in deference to Zorba and his fine hotel. I went to a local pub and drank some whisky, then I went to one of those new off-licences with the yellow fascias and bought a half-bottle there. I certainly wasn't going to pay Zorba's prices.

I sat at the table by the window and looked down on to the streets. The girls started to come out one by one like ragged little stars. They'd never stopped coming out, if it came to that. By some strange collective instinct they'd known they weren't at risk. I was almost tempted with my last fifty pounds to venture out on to the streets and find a little comfort. But Sarah was there, smiling at me from her frame, and I didn't want to let her down. Besides, the genius downstairs knew the case was closed. If I came back with a friend from the street, I couldn't face the smile on his face. In fact, I was looking forward to taking the smile off his face completely. I had counted the cockroaches downstairs, and noticed too how frequently the girls came in accompanied by a man, only to leave forty minutes later. That was why his register was always empty: he was doing the sort of bookings that don't get written down. I had the telephone in my hand and was about to pass through these observations to the relevant departments when Sarah caught my eye from her photograph. Why be vindictive? her face seemed to say, and I put the receiver back on its cradle. Ah, Mr Ashburton, you *are* a lucky boy, I thought. You'll never know quite how lucky you are. The next day I was back in Baildon.

A week later Frank phoned. Seed had bought a plea, he said.

'Don't really understand that he needs to, Frank,' I said. 'He's no murderer, after all.'

'All the same, the plea is murder in the first degree, multiplied by five.'

'That's insane,' I said. 'Strike half the doctors in the land off then, with their weekly euthanasia surgeries. He only did the same thing with consenting adults.'

'The Commissioner . . .'

'Never mind the Commissioner,' I said, 'what about justice? He didn't even dream it all up.'

'That's the point, Harry. Commissioner and wifey have a nice big sympathy vote at present, but if it turns out their daughter is a mass murderer by democratic vote . . .'

'Jesus, Frank. So a man's going to lose his life so that one pompous dickhead can be Minister for Culture?'

'Lose his life doesn't seem to be quite the way he'd put it, Harry. Or only to gain it anyway, according to him. That's in the Bible, isn't it?'

'More or less,' I said.

'Anyway he's bought a package, under the new death-penalty-with-rights deal. He wants to die by the administration of . . .'

'Five grammes of pure heroin.'

'My, but you're quick. And he's elected you to be his companion, for that last rite of passage. And also to receive the little urn containing his ashes afterwards.'

'If this is a joke Frank, it's a sick one.'

'No joke. One more trip on expenses for you down to London. Monday morning. He's elected not to go to trial. He gets administered on Tuesday.'

'You mean he dies.'

'You've been away too long, Harry, as I told you before. You don't know any of the right words these days.'

I went into the Self-Election Cells at Wandsworth on

Monday afternoon. Adam was there, dressed in white, smiling.

'You don't mind?' he said.

'Anything I can do,' I said. I realised suddenly how much I liked him.

'She'd said I should be laid to rest far to the north of the upright on the cross, you see. There wasn't any top part to the cross. That symbolised the resurrection for all of us. Baildon is perfect. I've looked at it on the map. Perfect. She knew whoever was provided would complete the scheme. She never had any doubt of that. I'd like to give you this,' he said, and handed me a copy of Emily Dickinson's poems.

'It was Sarah's copy. And that was her favourite there, number 277. I've put a marker in the page. Would you stay for dinner? They've arranged a very nice one. Wine and everything.'

'Yes Adam,' I said. 'I'll stay.'

The next day the doctor injected him at two o'clock. It didn't take long, for it was a massive overdose. I held him in my arms until he stopped breathing. There was a smile on his face. That should have made me feel better about the whole thing, I suppose, but it didn't. I hadn't realised until the evening that the date he had chosen was the 24th. 15 plus 9.

And a week after that the urn was delivered to me in Baildon. I've made a little corner for it in the garden, where he can at least get a bit of sun. I often go down there, as I will in a moment, with this book by Emily Dickinson, the one with Sarah's name inside the cover. I read to him you see.

Sarah smiles on us both from the window. I've turned her photograph round, so that it's facing outwards. It's her favourite I usually read:

> What if I say I shall not wait
> What if I burst the fleshly Gate –
> And pass escaped – to thee!
>
> What if I file this Mortal – off –
> See where it hurt me – That's enough –
> And wade in Liberty!
>
> They cannot take me – any more!
> Dungeons can call – and Guns implore
> Unmeaning – now – to me –
>
> As laughter – was – an hour ago –
> Or Laces – or a Travelling Show –
> Or who died – yesterday!

Underneath the Smile

Where did I learn to smile like that? I didn't come out of the womb smiling – I was screaming my head off, or so they tell me. And in those photographs of me as a young boy I stare out morose and quizzical. Not a smile in sight. Somewhere, though, before I hit puberty, I learned how to do it. Now watch. See the mirror? I say to that smile in there: What are you so happy about? And the smile says, I know I'm good, I know I'm moving, I know I'll succeed. Mr Smile means it too. God, how he means it.

There were times, I'll be honest with you, when that smile in the old silver-back looked a little ragged, even faded into straight lips and dead eyebrows, times when I had to go looking for the patron saint of mirrors. There must be one holy old man who tends these little frozen wells we drop our faces in, as though they were wishful pennies. There must be someone who bestows a blessing on our self-regard. But lately now the problem's largely solved. I've solved my life. I've paid off the mortgage on my smile. You're looking at a smiling man who's broken even.

Dick Shelley: singer/songwriter. Guitarist. You might

have caught me at the Shack on Kensington High Street on a Friday; or the Quarry in Soho on a Wednesday; or the Turk's Head in Shepherd's Bush on a Monday. I've played plenty of other places, of course, any number of city wine bars. But I'm through with crappy gigs now. I've done my last one. I've paid my dues. Why? Simple enough. I know I'm good, I know I'm moving, I know I'll succeed.

Some of you might recognise that slogan, those who've done MMM. For those who don't know, let me explain: MMM means Modern Mind in Movement, and my weekend with those masters of the spirit a few years back accounts for my present success. They shouted at me and abused me, even dragged me once across the floor. 'What's underneath the smile?' they screamed, until finally I screamed back at them, 'Fear. Failure and fear.' Then the modern saints connected my head up to my heart, and oiled the little motor of my soul. They sent me back into the world with gold in my veins and a song that goes, I know I'm good, I know I'm moving, I know I'll succeed. And now, as you can see, I have. What's underneath the smile these days? Another smile – an even brighter one. I'm smile all the way through. I gave my sadness to the winds and my fear to the birds. I arrived.

Look at the ducks there, splashing about in the pond. Nothing contradicts their duckness. I do love this little house. But I didn't always live in a house like this in Kew. It's been a long time coming, this arrival.

I suppose it started with Dylan. He was God, the great

white-faced clown up there making poetry out of the world's catastrophe. An acoustic guitar, that's all you needed. No band. No backing vocals. So I got the guitar and I learned the chords. Started writing my own songs too: 'Bye Bye Brooklyn' and 'New York's Musical Sunset'. Somehow I never could work Huddersfield into a song. Americans have a head start in this business. All they need do is climb aboard a Greyhound bus and they've launched a blues number. But if we get on a double-decker in Leeds, what happens? It's either Jake Thackray doing his lugubrious ironies, or England swinging like a pendulum do. I hate all that stuff. Dylan's a prophet up there: he sings and the world falls silent. He's Isaiah with a Martin six-string, and that's what I've always aimed for too. Now my album's out, you can judge for yourself.

So many pubs and clubs. So many bedsits. So many girls. If you're the man up there singing, you always catch their eye. If one of them's without a bloke, or fancies a change for the night, they ask for a request and give you the smile: 'Until It's Time for You to Go' was always a sure sign. If nothing came up from the floor, I used to sing the old Stephen Stills number, 'If You're Not With the One You Love, Love the One You're With'. That usually had somebody rummaging around in her handbag to see what she'd brought with her for the night. For a few years, I didn't really need a room of my own at all. And I hardly ever bought a meal.

You wouldn't credit how many recording contracts I've narrowly missed over the years. The most unbelievable cock-ups. Nearly there so many times, and then at the very last minute . . . Anyway, that's all resolved now. We're on our way. Maybe I'm glad the earlier deals didn't come off, come to think of it. I'd probably have produced a forgettable album that disappeared without trace. Now as it is, I've honed my talent till it shines. The age thing doesn't matter. Who does it matter to, for God's sake? Why do they keep turning out to see Dylan or Jagger if it's age that matters?

During my two years in Copenhagen playing at the Musikanten, I'll admit I seriously thought of packing it in. Penilla was comfortably off and had a beautiful flat in the centre of town. She said, if we married, I could have a couple of years just writing. I was bound to make it with something. But Scandinavian women, I don't know. Initially they seem so pale and mysterious, but you start to find out in the early hours of the morning about their secret melancholy. I wasn't sure myself what lay under my own smile at that point – hadn't done MMM. In fact, it was Penilla who raised the money for me to do MMM, come to think of it. Thought it might sort me out. But she wanted a child so badly. Given all the things I needed to do, that was out of the question (still is, in fact, until this breakthrough is complete).

I came back to London. Told Penilla I needed time to think. Two weeks later in Hammersmith I met Kirel. Three weeks later I moved in with her. She had a nice flat, company car, good job. She believed in me, believed in my talent. In fact, she lent me the money for my first Martin. Now, with one of those strung round my neck, there was nothing separating me from Dylan but the right spotlight on the right stage. After I left, it's true, Kirel started getting heavy with me about the loan. But I told her when I took the money I had no idea when I'd be able to repay it. When the zeroes start appearing at the end of my bank balance, I'll send her a grand. Well, maybe. Maybe not, if she writes any more letters like that last one.

The first week I had that guitar I was so excited that when I swung it from round my neck at Freddy's, as they were applauding, I hit myself right between the eyes with its wooden head. Blood started dribbling down my face. As I arrived back at the bar one of the punters says, 'You're bleeding, man.' 'Yeah,' I said, 'well, you've got to bleed in front of an audience, man.' Ah, rock and roll.

Managers. I've lost count, honestly. It's hard enough to write the material, and then get up there and belt it out while suits get pissed on sparkling wine, but if you have to do everything else yourself as well (writing to record companies, arranging gigs) well, it's hopeless. So you line yourself up with a manager. Then he's into you for 10, maybe 20 per cent. And what happens? Nothing. That's what. You're still doing the same gigs at the same places. No contract. With Harold, I didn't even see him for a month, then he arrives with one of his tarts at the wine bar one evening.

'Where've you been?' I said, tuning up.

'Thinking up the name that's going to make you famous,' he said. 'You're never going to get anywhere until you have a decent name. I had to go away and be alone to think. Nearly alone, anyway.'

'And?'

'I've got it.'

'Go on.'

'Happy Music.'

My hand made a sudden jerk and I snapped the top E-string.

'Happy Music?'

'It says everything about you.'

'Not very Dylan-like, is it?'

'Neither are you, mate.'

I invited Harold to leave at that point, and take his floozie with him, which he did. Never spoken to him since. Occasionally I've seen him out there, watching me from a safe distance, working out what he's thrown away in letting me go. You begin, perhaps, to see what I have been up against.

Let's take a little break. Let's get this black beauty out of the garage. BMW 325i. The wife's company car. She goes to work by public transport. Better for her nerves, I convinced her of that. So sometimes now on these summery afternoons, I take her out for a spin. Down to Richmond Park or along the river. With the hood down like this, can you think of anywhere else you'd rather be? One of the compensations of married life. It's not easy at the beginning, making do with the one woman. What's that on the CD-player? Glad you asked. As a matter of fact it's me. From my album, *Chicago*

Shimmer. Sounds pretty good, I think you'll agree. Solid music for driving through sunshine.

Angus Milner turned up shortly after Harold departed. Had some good times with Angus, over at his flat in Paddington. How the wine did flow. Never any need to bring a bottle – he already had plenty there. Angus had a job in some marketing company that obviously paid pretty well. Said he envied me, envied the life I'd chosen. There he was, making all this money and not knowing what to do with it. Strange relations with even stranger women. So I'd go over and see him whenever I fancied a drink or a meal, and he paid to set up the studio at my cousin Jack's flat – where in fact a lot of the original work for this album was done. We had a gentleman's agreement about it all, how when I started to make it he'd have a part of the action. When Angus was made redundant, though, he changed suddenly. There was an air of desperation about the man, garbling on about trying to get some return for his investment. The last thing I needed as I was breaking through was the likes of him hanging around to get a slice of me (everyone wants a slice, don't they?). Told Jack not to take calls from him any more and I didn't either. Finally, he gave up. I didn't invite him to the wedding.

Sometimes driving through Richmond Park like this, I imagine what it must have been like to be one of those kings out hunting round here. Maybe I could do a song about that. Hunting in a coupé? Riding a drophead? Might sound too English. Never could stand music that sounded English. I know that, technically speaking, I am English, but when I start to sing, I'm not. Music is the esperanto of the spirit.

Anyway, I finally had my breakthrough with Innisfree Records. The A and R scout (the daughter of the boss, in fact) heard me one night at the Moonraker's. Was impressed, and I fear a little more besides. She bought me a drink and expressed her surprise that I didn't already have a record out. I explained how often it had nearly happened, and then at the last minute there'd always been some bit of bad luck. Within a week I was signed. I hadn't understood, though, how much the music industry had been changing. The old days of advances to new artists are gone for good. Now the deal, as Brendan the boss explained to me, is that you produce the master tapes, which you then own, and you pay all the studio fees. The company covers the pressing costs and the CD box and handles distribution. What this actually came down to was that I had to raise £7,000 to see the album in the shops. Well, that would have been the end of it, I suppose, except for one thing: along came Lizzie.

I suppose I was Lizzie's first real boyfriend and let's face it, she went head-over-heels. This was serious passion. She's a talented girl too, in her own way. At twenty-two, to be one of the three main buyers for Goldilocks, is no mean achievement. Lizzie wanted me to marry her pretty badly. I told her I'd once made a vow to myself, a vow I could not break: I'd never marry until I had at least one album out. And at that moment in time there was one thing standing between myself and the fulfilment of this ambition: £7,000.

The first time she took me to her parents' house in Surrey, I thought there might have been some mistake. But no, that was the place all right. Detached house. Tennis court. Heated swimming pool. A three-part garage: a Mercedes, a Mercedes coupé and, wait for it, a Porsche 911 Turbo. The old man's got his own brokerage company in the City. He took an instant liking to me, did Lizzie's old man, plunged into my smile like a dolphin into a pool. I'd sit up late drinking whisky with him, and he told me how he envied me, in a way, choosing the road of freedom. Not being tied down by material things.

The engagement was announced. And Jeffrey (that's Lizzie's father) said he'd always planned on giving his daughter £10,000 anyway, whenever she married. So he was stumping it up a little in advance. I was back at the record company the following day with a cheque. Of course, £7,000 didn't cover all the costs, and by the time we were finished there wasn't much left out of the £10,000, but that's always the way with recording.

Anyway, we completed the album. It was officially released a week before we were married. We decided, or I decided, if the truth were known, not to marry in England – too many people I'd rather not see, to be honest. With the album coming out, there'd be too many old lags coming to collect, coming to stick their snouts in the trough. So the old man put his hand in his pocket again, and forked out for a villa in Spain for a month. Then, when we came back, we had our lovely little house in Kew to move into. For the moment Lizzie's salary covers the mortgage for that – until my music money really starts to pour in. In any case, we'd agreed – no more crappy gigs. They were doing nothing for my career at all. A little more movement on the album front and we're there. We'd best be steering homeward now before my youthful bride arrives back at the ranch.

He moves about methodically in the kitchen, like a man who knows where things are. He places the various items in the oven as he checks his watch. He lays the table with fussy precision. He opens a bottle of red wine, for he prefers red, and places it in the middle of the table with two polished glasses on either side of it. Then he puts *Chicago Shimmer* on the CD player, and sits in one of the large armchairs with his eyes closed. He does not notice her when she comes in. He only realises she is there when she switches off the CD. As he climbs out of the chair, his smile is changing up through its gears.

'Hi,' he says, as he kisses her on the cheek.

'Good day?' she says, unsmiling.

'Fine, yeah. Done a lot of work.'

'On what?'

'Oh, progressing songs, you know. Toning some versions up for performance.'

'You haven't been out then, Dick?'

'Little walk around the pond in the afternoon. Gave your regards to the ducks.'

'It's just that the bonnet of the car's warm.'

'Yes, well I did have a little drive, come to think of it. Just over to the record shop and back.'

'There's thirty more miles on the clock.'

He stares at her. He holds on to his smile, but he stares at her.

'You've started logging the speedo have you?'

She sits down on the chair by the window and starts to unbutton her pinstriped jacket.

'Get me a drink, would you?' she says. 'Dry white wine. Make sure it's chilled.'

He goes into the kitchen and opens a bottle of white. He pours out two glasses and carries them back in to his wife. She sips her drink for a moment and looks out through the window at the pond. She has the healthy blonde good looks of a daughter of stockbroker Surrey. There is nothing remarkable about her appearance, as she knows, but she is competently attractive. She understands how to wear make-up, and she knows how to buy clothes. Once, though it now seems a long time ago, she went through all the manoeuvres of passion, flinging back her head and moaning. She can't remember any more whether she was trying to fool him or herself. She feels she's been made to spend the whole of her life in front of a mirror. She is tired and feels thirty years older than she did twelve months before.

'It's been a year, Dick.'

He walks over to the CD-player and switches it on.

'Don't put it on again, for Christ's sake.'

He turns and looks at her. The smile is still there, but he is having to concentrate very hard on it now.

'Why not? Don't lose the faith, Lizzie. Remember the MMM . . .'

'Dick, your album's been out for a year. Our wedding gift was spent on paying for it. That was my dowry. The only person in the whole of Britain listening to it today is you. How many sales at the last count?'

'They say it's difficult to establish exactly.'

'How many?'

He looks down at the carpet and speaks quietly.

'Fifty.'

'Then we've paid everyone who bought the album two hundred pounds to listen to it.'

'You've a good head for figures, Lizzie.'

'Just as well, isn't it, Dickie? Though you always seem to be able to add up whatever it is you need. Whether it's from me or my daddy or . . . Kirel.'

Dick Shelley bites his lip.

'Did you read the letter that was in my pocket?'

Lizzie drinks the rest of the wine in the glass and then flicks her varnished fingernails against it.

'Do you owe her a thousand pounds, as she says?'

'Look, this is nothing to do with you. With us, I mean. It's all dead, all something that's gone.'

'Did you', Lizzie says, still tapping the wineglass, 'borrow a thousand pounds from Kirel for a guitar and then not pay her back?'

'Maybe.'

Lizzie lifts up her beige leather bag and opens it. She takes out her chequebook.

'What's her second name again?'

'Black. Kirel Black,' he says, still looking down.

She writes out the cheque and hands it to him.

'Make sure your old girlfriend gets this, would you? Anybody else while we're about it? Don't owe Angus anything, do you? Who bought all that equipment over at Jack's?'

'There was a gentleman's agreement,' Dick Shelley says, and turns his smile back on, full power. He feels they need a lift, feels they've both put their heads down a tunnel and it is time to pull them out again. Lizzie looks at that smile, the smile she thinks must have a switch attached to it somewhere, like any other room light, or the things that flicker on a CD-player. An off-switch. She remembers Angus, remembers the meals he bought for them both in Paddington, remembers Dick saying the first time they went to meet him, 'You won't need your purse.' So it was a gentleman's agreement, was it? Now that Angus is out of work, he presumably has plenty of time to reflect on friendship and loyalty. On money and gentlemen's agreements. Dick Shelley stands there smiling down at her. That smile she once said filled every room he entered. He walks over to her and puts his glass on the table. He kneels before her and places both his hands on her breasts, as he did that first night. She does not try to disguise it as she flinches away.

She stands up and holds out her empty glass towards him. Something flickers there momentarily in his face, she sees it, a flash of something in his eyes that is more like a blade than a smile.

'Fill it, if you don't mind. It's been a long day.'

He goes into the kitchen and brings out the bottle. He fills her glass, then he bows deeply.

'Whatever madame wishes.' And then the smile comes back on like floodlights over a football pitch. She decides that today at last she will find out what's underneath it.

'It has been a year, Dick,' she says, 'since your album was released and we were married. A whole year. You've dropped all the gigs because they were beneath you. Doing nothing for your career, you said. Each day I set off to work by bus and tube so I can earn the money to pay the mortgage and buy the food and fill up the BMW with petrol. And what do you do, Dick?'

'I keep the house tidy,' he says with a confidence she's not expecting. 'Which you're not very good at yourself. I do the shopping. I do the washing. I do the ironing. I cook the food. I serve the drinks. I do the washing up.'

She looks at him and sips her wine.

'You're an expensive housekeeper, Dick, if that's all you are.'

'I also happen to be an artist,' he says. 'Or had you forgotten?'

Lizzie fills up her glass again with the cold white wine. She's not eaten all day. She is beginning to feel reckless.

'Tim from work drove me to a meeting today. As we were driving along in his car, he played me his tape. It was good, really good. Why didn't you go on with it? I asked him. Do you know what he said, Dick? He said, "You've got to understand that everybody was out there with a guitar strung round his neck. We all thought we were Dylan. At a certain age, you have to face facts. In that world, if you haven't got somewhere by the time you're thirty, you most likely never will." '

She is looking through the window. The ducks have gone from the pond. She wonders where it is they go to. She carries on talking without turning round.

'You're forty-three this year Dick. You're only six years younger than my daddy . . . I used to think how exciting it would be to be married to an artist.'

'Changed your mind then?' he says.

'I'm not sure you are one really,' she says. 'You're just a failed star, and that's different. You're just one of the millions of stars that didn't manage to shine brightly enough.' She turns from the window to face him. 'You're going to have to get a job, Dick.'

'We agreed about all that,' he says coldly.

'Whatever we agreed,' she says, emptying the rest of the bottle into her glass, 'whatever we *once* agreed about all that, I'm not keeping you any more. Anyway, you're too old to be a toyboy, and I'm still too young to need one.'

She walks over to him as he drinks his wine warily, not

taking his eyes off her. She brings her face within a foot of his and cocks her head to one side.

'You had it all set up didn't you, Dick Shelley? Except I think you'll find the audience is missing. Even in bed you act as though there's a film crew in the room making a video. The truth is, when it comes right down to it, you're no good, you're not moving, you won't succeed.'

His fist makes contact with a force that takes him by surprise. She is thrown back against the table and the wineglass crashes on the wall and shatters. There is a streak of wet where it meets the paint. As she turns towards him from the floor, he can see the blood mingling with her blonde hair and dripping on to her white silk blouse. That won't come out.

'Oh Christ,' he says, 'I'm sorry. Sorry sorry sorry.' He reaches down to her, but she slaps his hand away.

'I wasn't hitting you,' he says. 'Not you, whatever you just said. I didn't hit you. I hit everyone else. Those bastards at the record company who conned me and ripped me off. The sneering manager of every third-rate wine bar in London. The arseholes in the City I had to grin in front of, while I played the drivel they requested. Everybody,' he says, beginning to cry, 'the whole fucking world. But not you.'

She stands up and looks in the mirror. She is a beaten wife. That's a new experience anyway, she thinks. At least marriage has given me something novel to brood about. She does not cry. She walks silently from the room.

In front of the mirror himself now, moving into it as

though it's a bed she's climbed out of a moment before, he sees a sad face, the face of a stranger with tears in his eyes, hair going grey, skin starting to sag a little. Somewhere, deep down in that frozen well, a smile has finally disappeared.

A Compass in the Dark

On the last leg of the transatlantic flight from New York to London, Hugh Martindale stared through the window and saw the moon's dim head shrouded in a caul of mist. Below him St George's Channel was scattered with the navigation lights of tankers and freighters and ferries. The hills of Wales were only a few miles off now, as the plane drilled on through the howl of the weather. The food had all long ago been served and most of the drinks long finished; except for the few who never finished, who made mute masonic signs to the stewardesses on their swaying journeys between the flight deck and the tail. Regulation smiles remained firmly fixed in place above those uniforms, as they bent in solicitude to check whatever cravings still remained unassuaged.

Twenty minutes later the captain's well-schooled voice informed them that London was cold and damp. England's chilly drizzle had returned on cue. Hugh didn't mind. He'd be glad to be back again for a while, even though he did love Manhattan; loved the symmetric grid of its streets, the snappy *brio* of its big hotels. And its art galleries too, particularly the ones that put on exhibitions of his work. He picked up the copy of *a/r/t* for the fifth time and started rereading the review.

Compass-Room *by Hugh Martindale*

This installation confirms that Hugh Martindale is now undoubtedly one of Britain's most exciting artists.

At the centre of a darkened room stands a compass in its binnacle. All around the edges lights flicker on and off, and it is only gradually that we come to understand what is going on in the shadowy space around us, the space of uncertainty we are obliged to move through. For the binnacle turns round slowly and inexorably, completing a 360-degree circuit every nine minutes, while the lights around the edges of the room are paired, and flash in synchronised though separate sequences, just as the lights on harbours and buoys do, for navigational identification. The whole room is alive with movement, orientation, and warning; only the compass itself at the centre remains unmoved, fixed on its target. And yet it is moving all the time, of course, as it hunts for magnetic north. As metaphor . . .

The plane put down at last and skirred to a standstill, juddering as the retro engines whined. They all unclipped from seat belts; shuffled, stretched and yawned, then jostled one another as they pulled their luggage from the lockers. He stepped finally into the cold beyond the fuselage. It always felt like such a long and breezy walk through those antiseptic corridors. Then it was passport control. The young man gazed at his photograph. Hugh was half-fogged with exhaustion, but still registered when the eyes flicked up, as always, in an expression of practised incredulity. Then baggage, customs and a taxi home.

The cab arrived finally at the converted Victorian warehouse, a little downriver from St Katharine's Dock. Hugh let himself in and rode the silent lift to the top floor. Inside his apartment he flicked the monitor quickly to check that his XJS, down in the underground car park, had remained untouched. There was no sign of interference, not that he had expected any, for this was a secure building. He was seriously tired after the journey, and ten minutes later he lay asleep in bed.

Next day he rose at dawn, his body still snarled in transatlantic time. The river frontage of his apartment was glass from floor to ceiling, and he stood there with a coffee in his hand, watching the Thames as it converted the steely greys of the sky into its own glassy movement. He walked over and stood in front of the prize piece of his collection: the Ben Nicholson white relief. Around the walls were other pictures and designs in various states of abstraction.

He sat down in front of his television and pressed a few buttons on the monitor. He had set the video to record his interview with Melrose before he left. The little film started with shots of his installation in America and the exhibition now showing in Yorkshire, which he was due to attend that day. Melrose walked around them, with his hair quiffed luxuriously back, and a well-rehearsed look of intelligent appraisal on his face. When he finally turned his large brown eyes towards the camera, he asked soulfully, 'Hugh Martin-dale. Is he, as some believe, amongst our greatest living artists; or might he be, as his critics insist, simply the curator of his own exhausted themes? I interviewed him earlier this year in an attempt to find out.'

Hugh pressed the fast-forward button so as to skip the remaining biographical information. He keyed back into himself as he stared up briefly at a distant part of the studio, and began to speak.

'Many people have the wrong notion about what I'm doing. I have no interest in demolishing tradition, none at all. I simply carried on with the tradition at the point where I joined it. You won't find a greater enthusiast than me for the big painters, for Rembrandt or Velasquez, but that time's gone for good. It would be as absurd to try to paint the way they do as it would be to wear their clothes or sleep in their beds. I would say that the last definitively great canvas painter is Picasso, but what you are seeing there are the death throes of one form of art. Magnificent but terminal. In the desperate metamorphoses and savage inventiveness of Picasso's pictures, you are watching six hundred years of life finally come to a close. And after that the easel's finished for good. Oh, I know there's the odd pocket of resistance here and there, but it's a bit like Japanese soldiers popping up on islands in the Pacific years after the war had ended. They just hadn't noticed that the battle was over.

'I think it was Le Corbusier who first said that the cars and planes, even the grain silos, of our era arrive at forms which are so beautiful because they solve the problems of function with both economy and grace. And that's my starting point. I take off from the effective designs of industrial and post-industrial society, because I can never rival them from my own imagination. Picasso's minotaurs look so miserable because they know they've already been condemned to extinction. They're finished. If I start from a compass in a machine casing, or a computer processing its calculations, that's because these objects, these agencies, are the real companions of my life here and now. These are the shapes that fill my world, as they do yours too, I think, David.'

The camera took in the full-frontal face of David Melrose, his smile quizzical though not unsympathetic, as he spoke the final words.

'And for those who cannot get across the Atlantic, but wish to judge Martindale's work for themselves, *The Engines Weep Numbers* will be showing at the Defoe Gallery in York from the beginning of January.'

Later in the morning he phoned Sue.

'Just back last night. Late last night.'

'How was it?'

'Good, actually. It's going well over there. How are the girls?'

'They're fine. When shall I tell them that they'll get to see you?'

'As soon as I'm back from Yorkshire. A gallery up there's showing *The Engines Weep Numbers*.'

'I know, Hugh. I saw it on the box. You should tell us when you're appearing. Your daughters would like to know when their famous daddy's going to be on TV, then they can boast about it at school.'

'Sorry,' he said. 'It's just that it always seems a bit self-important somehow, going round telling people when you're going to be on. But give them my love. I'll be round before the end of the week, promise. Bearing gifts from afar.'

After lunch he drove up to York in his Jaguar. He had missed that car while he'd been in the States, missed the faultless glide of acceleration delivered from its automatic transmission. Shortly before he arrived he caught the piece on *Kaleidoscope* about the installation at Defoe's. Essentially positive, though with some little jeers that struck him as unnecessary. Later he was interviewed by the *Yorkshire Post* in a cluttered office in the gallery, to the side of the main exhibition space. He had grown so used to being interviewed, it wasn't something he thought about in advance any more.

'Why do engines weep numbers?' the nervous young man asked.

'Why not ask them?' he said. 'They could probably give you a more accurate answer than I can. But maybe it's because they're decoding the mysteries of what we call creation. Maybe it's because they're approaching the singularity, and can't halt the momentum of their own calculations. Maybe it's because they're finally coming to understand us. Wouldn't you weep?'

Then later he walked around his own work, as the printouts chattered into trays, and the screens flashed technicolor diagrams. He had forgotten how good it was.

Next day he drove over to Bradford, where, a quarter century before, it had all begun. That's where he had been at art school, before going on to the RCA in London. And that's where he'd met Peter Sansom, and Patsy, whom he was taking out to dinner that evening. He had made a point of keeping in touch once or twice a year. A card, if nothing else. It seemed important, somehow.

He drove round and round the town, studying its changes. Old Methodist chapels were now luxurious curry houses, and the stone was everywhere beige, the colour of scrubbed millstone grit. But surely it had been black when he had been here? He still remembered it that way, or had his memories melded into the photographs of the place, and his own mythic images of Worstedopolis, all those ghostly wool combers and handloom weavers that the machines had put out of work for ever? He parked the car at the top of Dalcross Grove and walked to the centre of the little bridge over the old railway. This line used to run to Blackpool through Preston, and he had lived two houses down: he could see the back garden now, tidier than it had ever been when they had lived there. He had sat on that wall and listened to the steam engines breathing deeply as they paced themselves for the gradient. To the other side was the mill where his father had worked. It was a dead mill now, a dead mill and a dead father too. He walked through its stinking ruins. Perhaps in a few more centuries it would gain the sepulchral splendour of Fountains Abbey, riddled in the shroud of its own passing. He stopped at one of the shattered windows. A single clump of wool trailed down, with a flash of blue dye running through it. Cobalt.

He drove through West Bowling, staring up and down its few remaining snickets, and looked closely at the occasional mill building left standing, metal claws still hanging by chains from the upper-storey cranes, but with cargoes of nothing moving through them now, only the wind. He stopped down Hall Ings to look up at those Italianate warehouses which Bradford's self-made millionaires had needed to build, to create some Renaissance splendour up here, under the black skies of the industrial north.

Finally he checked into the hotel, showered, changed, observed his slim figure in the mirror, took a drink from the minibar, and phoned Peter. Patsy answered.

'Hello, you.' It had only happened once between them, while her relationship with Peter flicked from the on to the off button in the early days, but he could never hear her voice without remembering the turbulence of her body beneath him that night.

'Pete's not here actually, Hugh. Out sketching. Term starts again next week, so he's making the best of it. Always does.'

'You're both coming tonight anyway.'

'I can't, Hugh, sorry. I'm really sorry, I did want to – it would have been lovely to see you again after all this time. But the only person who can do some baby-sitting round here is sick. Tina's still only twelve. I don't like leaving her alone at night . . .'

'I'm sorry,' he said, 'I was looking forward to seeing you again. Still, some other time. Pete's coming, though?'

'Oh yes, wouldn't miss it for the world.'

So after he had hung up, he called down and changed the restaurant booking. Now there would only be the two of them.

Peter Sansom was crouching on the hill above Halifax, his sketchbook held in his crooked left arm, as the pencil moved slowly over the white paper. Ahead was a row of cottages, half of them derelict, set against the furze and heather of the rough-cast hill behind them. The contrasts here were alert with all the possibilities he liked to work on when he was back home.

It had started with Hopper. After all the art-school blather, the gleeful hype and ballyhoo, that he had once shared as a student with his old friend Hugh Martindale, Peter had sensed an emptiness gnawing at him. Those huge reliefs made up of bobbins and spindles, the worsteds deconstructed into noils and tops; enormous canvases of black looming shapes. *Enoch Hammers*, he'd called that series, and all of this had somehow been a part of the revolutionary murmur of the times back there. The strikes and sit-ins, the occupation of the central building. Even then, he'd heard himself mutter, Do we really think they'll close capitalism down because a few art schools are preaching sedition? Reefers in the college lavatory. Parties where it was obligatory to go into at least one bedroom with at least one woman you'd not known longer than an hour. It had taken him a while to realise that all this was surf on a temporary wave, not liberation, certainly not enlightenment. And, more to the point, not work. Not any real work that might last. He'd realised then how much he wanted to do some work that would last.

No, it had started with Hopper. He could still remember the first time he had ever stood before one and thought silently to himself, *This is it*. Not that he could have defined *it*, couldn't then and couldn't now, but this was definitively it. What he had been looking for: a way of approaching a city, and the land around it; a way of approaching the country, and the buildings upon it; a way of portraying the mild desolation of humanity, caught out nakedly living among its own creations, staring at them as though they might have retained some runic secret as to how all this had started, and where it might be heading. All of the daubs and ready-mades and agitprop confections lost their interest for him there and then, in that single moment of recognition. He knew only that he'd have to spend his life pursuing this.

So at the college now they called him Prairie Pete, though he wondered how many of them would even have known that his compositions and his brushwork had received their start in life from a study of Hopper had he not pointed it out to them himself beforehand. He was the department's anachronism. Sometimes referred to, contemptuously, as the Ancient of Days. When he occasionally made his applications to other art schools for other jobs, he knew it was futile before he even began, for he was wedded to the dead tradition. He was one of the leftovers, who'd still not seen the neon writing on the wall.

There was one window he was drawing that could take a woman's shape. Women were the great sacrificial gifts of Hopper's city, for which the city had no real use, since it had no real altars, unless you were to count the unmade beds in cheap hotels, or the service counters in banks, where they sat behind glass screens to receive the wealth that men of all shapes and sizes brought as offertory gifts, or those endless tables in the typing pool where their stockinged legs would cross and then uncross themselves, while the ghost of sex attended that collective whisper. Then there were dawn litanies at open windows as the noisy, crowded vacancy outside got on its way. How they offered their nakedness to the city, which looked on unblinking through symmetric windows.

It struck him that he could put Patsy there, naked except for a slip, a black slip to contrast with the white flaking paint, her breasts startling the glazed rectangle out of its complacency. He had painted her so many times, each and every part of her, that he no longer had to ask her to pose, though sometimes he still did, and sometimes she still agreed. Another mystery: how hormones had their own long seasons, their awakenings and hibernations. He looked at his watch. It was time to go, or he'd be late. The light was dying now completely in any case. Shadows lost their interest without a potent light to discipline their edges.

On the bus coming back, he stared down from the top deck on to the ossified parks around the eges of town; the slimed-over ponds, pocked with refuse and rotting supermarket trolleys. Hopper had captured, entirely without sentimentality, the immense weariness of cities, the great sigh of exhaustion you can hear whenever you are left alone in them for a moment. All he was trying to do was to capture the same thing, but here in the West Riding of Yorkshire, instead of in America. Peter's great nostalgic project, as he had heard one of his colleagues once describe it behind his back at the college. But he reckoned they were the ones who were nostalgic: nostalgic for Dada, for surrealism, for Tristan Tzara and the cabaret in Zürich, nostalgic for the hammer of an art so radical and so utterly anarchic that it would clang against the side of the world with a clamour loud enough to deafen the moneyed conscience of the bourgeoisie for ever. It had all been done, though, over and over again, and the only difference it had ever made to the bourgeoisie was that they now had a better technique for advertising cigarettes and motor cars. Anyway, he knew one thing for sure: you couldn't inherit a revolution, any more than you could inherit a tradition. You had to earn them both through the lifetime of struggle that was your own technique.

When he arrived back, Patsy was making their daughter's tea.

'Your famous friend phoned,' she said. 'He's expecting you for dinner at seven.'

'Dinner?' Tina said incredulously.

'That's what they call tea down south, love.'

Hugh was sitting at the hotel window staring out at the town hall. Its tower was based on the *campanile* of the Palazzo Vecchio in Florence, and these days they lit it up at night. They hadn't done that when he'd lived there. The phone rang and the receptionist told him that his guest had arrived.

Peter was three or four inches shorter than Hugh, and as they briefly embraced Hugh realised that his friend's hair had largely disappeared since their last meeting. Only cropped grey bristle on either side was left, making the gold earring all the more prominent. Hugh pointed to it.

'The gypsies made me wear it,' Peter said, grinning a little shyly, 'said they'd make off with me otherwise.'

'Suits you, Pete, a hint of that raffish look you had all those years ago, when I first clapped eyes on you. You're still wearing the same linen suit as well, by the look of it. I recognise that dab of paint there on the shoulder. Chrome yellow. I think that was out of my tube. The Tate'll have that, if you don't watch it. Part of our heritage. And now you have wire-rimmed specs as well. You could almost pass for Brecht in Berlin in the 1920s.

'How's Patsy? The kids?'

'They're fine, all fine. Patsy's sorry she couldn't make it. Sue and the twins?'

'Fine. I'll get to see them all when I get back. Spend the day there. Came straight up for the exhibition. Here's the prospectus, by the way. And also the last issue of *a/r/t*. Has a review of my latest, over in New York.'

Peter took them from him, and they walked through into the restaurant. Hugh couldn't help noticing how crumpled his old friend was. He felt a little guilty at being so immaculately turned out, but it had become a habit these days. Twenty-five years before, they had both dressed as Peter was dressed. But that was then, and this was now.

The food and wine were ordered, and when everything was settled, they sat and stared at each other in silence for a few seconds. Peter smiled and spoke first.

'You know, Hugh, you look younger now than you did when we were at college together. What is it?'

'Sunshine?'

'Money, I think, mate. You need money to buy sunshine like that. Round these parts, folks just go off to Benidorm for a fortnight and come back looking like boiled lobsters. Two weeks later, they're exactly the same as before. But you've got one of those grainy tans that seems to go all the way through, like the lettering inside Blackpool rock. You've got to be doing something right to look like that in the middle of winter.'

The wine had arrived, and Hugh started pouring it.

'I'm not complaining, Pete. How's life at the college these days?'

'Oh, not bad. I'm the last custodian of the old curiosity

shop. I think they only keep me on to remind everyone of the forgotten glories of empire. A man who draws, and then paints from his drawings, would you believe it? A fellow still committed to the pictorial and figurative inheritance, God help us all. Old Prairie Pete, the moorland nutter. Cheers anyway.'

'Cheers. You know what I think: your work should have more recognition. If you only spent some serious time in London . . .'

'Last occasion I was down in London, I spent a week at the V and A. I'd arranged to use the library down there. Turned up at opening time every day. Stayed till it closed. In the middle of the week, I'm grafting away and suddenly this voice starts up behind me. Not any old voice. The voice of someone who's once been garrotted, but let off right at the very last minute. Vocal chords all twisted into a braid. I turned round and said SHHHHH! The voice immediately goes up an octave. This time I stood up, turned round, and had a good look at the bugger. There's this stick insect with a bonsai haystack for a barnet, warbling away at the top of his voice to two men in pin-stripe suits. So I say, "Will you for Christ's sake, shut up. Can't you see people here are trying to get some work done?"

'An assistant comes mincing down on me and whispers, whispers, mind you, "You can't talk to him like that." Why not? I said. "That's the Director." No, you can keep London, Hugh. It's all yours.'

'When were you down?' Hugh asked, as casually as he could.

'Oh, last year sometime.'

'Should have phoned me.'

'I tried,' Peter said, evidently lying. 'There was no answer. You were probably off installing something in Australia.' Their first course was being put before them. 'Anyway, here's to you, and your success.'

'And to you, and the success you deserve.' They started to spoon soup and break bread.

'I saw you on Melrose's programme, by the way,' Peter said, 'and unless I'm losing my faculties altogether, I had the feeling you were saying that my sort of stuff's done for. Terminally done for.'

Hugh looked uneasy. He put down his spoon, and took up his glass. 'I was trying to define where I'm at, that's all. I think there's something about Melrose that brings out the worst in everyone. He's very, I don't know, *seductive*.'

'He spoke very highly of you, all the same. But I did have the distinct impression that canvas art was a gonner, in your view. That it was all over and done with. That I am, as they say, flogging a dead horse. Or were you unfairly edited?'

'Well, no, I suppose that's what I do believe really. That's why I do what I do, when it comes down to it. That's what I'm about. I mean, it doesn't have to be Francis Bacon's studio for ever, does it?'

Peter saw the studio in his mind, with its one bare light bulb and its smears and splodges of paint besmirching every wall, as though a bomb had exploded in an abattoir, and the splatterings of intestine and brain still clung to whatever surface had received them. And at the centre an easel with a canvas mounted upon it, as if the room were still that of Memling or Van Eyck. He loved Bacon's studio.

'The foul rag and bone shop of the heart,' Peter said, sipping his wine.

'I mean, it doesn't have to be that way, does it?'

'No,' Peter said thoughtfully, 'you could have Mondrian's Manhattan studio instead.' He had visited it on his one trip to the States. While he was inside, it seemed as though the hygiene of mathematics had conquered the rainbow. 'Or there's the assembly floor of those hi-tech warehouses in Camden.'

'You want screams, do you? You actually need meat blurring in agony? Illustrations of Dante, and all that stuff.'

'I seem to remember Dante had a paradise as well as an inferno. I'm not demanding anything at all, as a matter of prescription. I just want the signature of the struggle, that's all. I want whatever medium anyone works in to be the signature of a struggle with the realities they've confronted. And I always know when it's there in someone's work, and when it isn't. I don't think getting other people, however skilled, to put everything together for you is much of a way to form that signature. Whether it was Henry Moore doing it towards the end, or Damien Hirst doing it right at the beginning, getting someone else to kill that sheep and install it for him. For myself, I decided the world's too much of a gift not to want to include it. To turn down so much information, so much achievement, strikes me as a bit churlish.'

'We don't live in an age of paint, Pete, we live in an age of machines and electronics.'

'Fine, so use them. But do we start from life, then, or machines? I'm still wrestling with the riddles I find in the human face. I know all the riddles are there. Hopper's faces seem sometimes like tragic masks, but at least they're never mechanical. Real experience has always formed the mask, somewhere back down the line. Machines aren't condemned to death, are they? Even computers don't weep.'

'They weep numbers,' Hugh said, pouring the last of the wine out between them, and pointing to the prospectus Peter had placed on the floor beside him.

'Oh, right.'

On the way home on the bus, Peter read the essay in *a/r/t*, and the prospectus from the Defoe Gallery. When he arrived back, he let himself quietly into the garage that he used as a studio. He had removed all the old metal panels from the roof and replaced them with clear corrugated sheets, to catch whatever sun arrived. He switched on the light and stood looking at the long canvas he had finished the week before. It was a portrait of the disused RAF base in East Yorkshire, with its derelict barracks and blasted hangars. There was a certain heroism in those unadorned runways, rotting slowly under the weather's clock. That way of painting the moorland grass round about he had certainly learned from Hopper. But the brushwork had been changing over the years. It was his own now, and he knew it. He had made it his own. It was all growing more abstract too, but that was something else the people at college didn't understand: he had no objection to abstraction, none at all, as long as it grew naturally from the work, as long as it came out of the struggle. But there was a bogus abstraction, imposed as a schema from the outset, and that he detested. That was all gesture and skim, and he wanted nothing to do with it. Cézanne's mountain was abstract because it inevitably became a study of colour and form and composition, more intense with each new canvas. But his own eyes met the mountain every day. You only had to think of him telling someone else to go out and do his seeing for him to realise how absurd it would be. If a hireling can do the labouring for you, then you're in the construction industry. An artist's work couldn't be so easily escaped. It was relentless, treacherous and obscure, as you fathomed an unpredictable progress inch by inch, with only your own skill and integrity to fall back on. He switched off the light and locked the door, then went into the house.

The next morning Hugh Martindale checked out of his hotel, and drove back over to West Bowling. Something had been troubling him, though he couldn't think why. He parked as he had done the day before, at the top of Dalcross Grove. This time he took his Polaroid camera from the boot.

He always kept it there along with his Nikon, for he often liked to see an image develop. He walked back over the stone bridge and into the ruins of the mill, until he stood once more before the broken glass and that piece of dirty wool with its ancient streak of cobalt blue dye. He pointed the Polaroid and pressed the shutter. The camera hissed and slicked out a square piece of card. Its surface at first was a blind film of milky white, but as he walked back to the car it was already flowering into colour in his hand. He laid the picture on the passenger seat and drove off.

He would glance at it from time to time, between the car's grand surges of speed. For some reason it had started him thinking and calculating and adding together units of time. How old had he been when the last men left the mill? How long had one solitary piece of wool been fluttering there in the wind? And how many years had passed since that sheep had died?

The Pig Man of Gadara

It had been a bad year for pigs as it was. I found myself thinking again and again of Cornwall. No point denying that the fishing had been good there, though a man would have to be seriously hungry to eat mackerel day after day. I made a decent enough living in my little boat, but the bone ache got worse and the herbs I took didn't help any more. I went east in search of sun and trade.

There was plenty of sun in Palestine and plenty of trade too through the cities of the Decapolis. I settled at Gadara because at least I could wander down to the waters of Galilee and watch the sails flick in the wind. Sometimes if I closed my eyes I could imagine I was back in the mouth of the Fowey.

I got my pigs at what I thought a keen enough price. It was only later I discovered there might be anything complicated about raising pigs in Galilee. I knew nothing at this point, you see, except that here was a busy part of the Roman Empire with plenty of mouths to feed. There was a temple near by and the Romans had a lot of use for pork around their temples. It was only when I tried to pass the time of day with one of the local Jewish fishermen that it struck me things might not be as simple as I'd originally hoped. I had to start studying.

There was such an avidity for law among them. I've come across many gods in my travels and I listen patiently as some acolyte tells me how, on revealing himself to the high priest or an ancient holy man, such and such a god explained the colours of the rainbow, or permitted a vision of the deepest ocean, or vouchsafed the secret of perpetual fecundity. But there when a man went up a mountain, he came down carrying half the mountain with him, Shalt and Shalt Not neatly chipped out over every surface.

So it was I learned that their deity, having made all the animals, then forbade the eating of half of them. One would have thought he could have either forbidden the eating of any of them, or only made ones that could be eaten. As it is, it's a recipe for dissension, a menu for conflict.

Anyway, here I was in Galilee with my pigs, surrounded by a people who thought the animals unclean and anyone tending them even uncleaner. The one Jew I got to know shouted at me (for he wouldn't come within twenty feet) that were he actually to touch me, ritual purification would be required of him for the better part of a week. I'm a hardened traveller, but I found this wounding. The Cornish are a flinty lot and shy of what's called intercourse, but none of them ever felt the need to wash me off after shaking hands.

Then there was the demoniac. When I first found out about him, I realised that the glint in the eye of the man who sold me the herd might not have been merely the reflection of the gold coins in my hand, after all. There was a graveyard near where the pigs wandered, not a graveyard of the sort you'd find in Britain, but large white tombs hewn from the rock. One evening I was looking out over the lake when the wailing started. A gaunt, keening sort of sound that seemed to slice into your soul.

I went up there to look and saw a man in among the tombs, naked and covered in faeces, chained to the rocks but thrashing his arms and legs about so that blood was mixed with the other stuff. My stomach turned to look at him. As I approached, he stopped suddenly to stare, alert as an animal.

'What do you want in this foreign land?' the voice said with an air of command I'd not expected.

'Peace for my aching bones,' I said.

'You'll find no peace here. Begone.'

With that the wailing and shrieking started up again. The locals told me (from a distance) that this was the man with a demon, though some said it was many demons. He was chained up to prevent him destroying himself, they said. Unchain him and let him get on with it, I said.

Anyhow, that's how things stood before the local temple closed down. They decided there was not sufficient clientèle to justify the expense. They were rationalising temple worship through the towns of the Decapolis. Very rational people, the Romans. They're even rational about their superstitions.

Now I looked at my pigs, surrounded by Jews who wouldn't eat them or share a cup of wine with their owner; Romans who'd stopped buying them because they'd moved temple; and a demoniac in among the tombs. Begone, he'd cried, and I was beginning to think that was the best advice I'd received so far.

I didn't have much to do. I grew fond of the pigs. They were at least — as far as I could see — free from prejudice. Surprisingly capable of affection too. Then the rumours started. Another holy man was coming down the lake to preach the end of the world. The enthusiasm in those parts for laws was only matched by a great delight in all schemes of worldly cataclysm. As far as I could make out, it was thought that a Messiah would come soon to set the world to rights, which meant, as I understood it, the locals back on top and the Romans at the bottom (with maybe one pig farmer from Cornwall underneath the lot). Every time a healer or an exorcist came through the region, their eyebrows would twitch and their lips quiver. More signs of the kingdom. Another date clocked up towards the finale.

I placed myself slightly to the east of the tombstones so I could see this one for myself. Great crowds gathered and all the shrivelled and mangled, the lame and diseased, the leprous and the amputees stood in a line down the mountain. And as he came down, in a long white shift with his people streaming behind him, he touched them one by one and one by one they walked and gleamed and smiled. The people were cheering. I stood up myself, though I had meant to crouch in my hole, well out of the way of swinish epithets, of which I'd heard enough to last me a lifetime. And how my legs hurt. I thought, I who believe in nothing but the price of things, I thought I might go and stand in line myself and be touched. If the blind could be made to see, surely this ice in my bones could be thawed a little. Then that voice started up.

'What have I to do with thee, Jesus, thou son of God most high? I beseech thee, torment me not.'

It was the demoniac, weeping and gibbering. And he went right up to him, that healer, closer than anyone else but the chainmaker ever went.

'What is thy name?' he said.

'Legion,' came the crowds of voices, a whole snakepit of cries as though the fellow had a Roman circus in his belly.

'Don't send us into the deep,' cried the voices, 'not into the cold deep water. Let us go and find a home in the herd of pigs there.'

The healer turned and looked at my pigs. I was already trying to make myself heard above the shouting. 'Wait,' I said, 'wait, those are my . . .'

But it was too late. He gave some sign, some indisputable command, and a wild white flurry filled the air between the man possessed and my herd. It was all alive with icy whistles. It was like a snowstorm off the Needles – here in the middle of Galilee in the sun. The pigs spun around as though I were beating them, then off on their little trotters down the hill and into the lake. Drowned. Every single one of them.

The demoniac sat still now, shivering. They cleaned him up and he seemed as sane as I was. The people gathered round and praised the power of the Almighty, and the man told us not to wait any longer for the kingdom, since it was here inside the heart of each one of us. The people shouted out their hallelujahs, then they asked the healer to leave. Quickly. To go as far away as he could manage. If it was pigs today, it might be sheep tomorrow. Then he'd have the fish out of the lake. Whose livelihood would be safe?

I worked my way back to Cornwall with the Lebanese girl I married in Biblos. Round here these days they worship Cernunnos, the antlered god with green veins who brings back the spring each year. Myself, I've seen enough of religions. A man can live without them. Something happened though a few weeks back. My little farmhouse is up on the hill overlooking the Fowey. I can keep an eye on my sheep from here and make sure the boy sets out in the boat each day when he should.

An old fellow landed with a young man to help him. They put a crossed staff into the ground as a marker at the estuary mouth and came up through the village. I met him the next day and he said to me, 'I believe you are the one who was in Palestine.'

'I was,' I said, 'many years ago.'

'Did you ever hear of a man named Jesus?'

'Yes,' I said. 'He drowned my pigs.'

The old fellow looked at me. One old man looked hard at the other.

'Did you ever hear what became of him?' he said.

'I heard that he went to Jerusalem and broke the money-changers' tables in the temple. The man was bad news for business, I'll tell you that much. Then someone told me as I was setting sail from Lebanon that he'd upset the Romans too, and they crucified him.'

'He has come back from the dead,' he said quietly.

'My pigs haven't.'

I had him and his assistant for dinner that night. There's not much in the way of social life in these parts. If you invite a Cornishman to dinner, he brings a knife. Joseph was his name. From Arimathea. He told me terrible stories of the goings on over there. Now the Romans have razed the Jerusalem temple to the ground. I had to get up a number of times from the table to ease the pain in my bones. Joseph asked about it, he was most solicitous.

'It's funny,' I said, 'I went all that way to cure this pain in my bones. The one time I might have had my cure, I ended up lamenting pigs instead. Don't even like pork much. Stick to sheep now.'

'This lamb's nice,' the young man said.

'Good,' I said. 'My own recipe.' (My young Lebanese bride found either me or the climate too cold and left many years ago. We never could understand one another.)

On the day they set sail the old fellow went in for more embracing than I care for. He muttered what I suppose were his benedictions. Aramaic, if I'm not mistaken. I still remember the sound of it from my time around those Galilean caves. Then their little boat was off on the outgoing tide. There's been a small change in the weather since they left, if I'm not mistaken. The pain in my bones hasn't been giving me so much gyp.

An Old Man in Florence

'They took my prostate out last year. I leak, I'm afraid. Not very hygienic. Inadvertent squirts.'

Eyes rimmed red, but behind the thick convex lenses of his tortoiseshell spectacles, they were no redder than many a bank manager's or politician's. When he came back into the room, there were damp splodges on his green trousers, miniature lakes on the topography of his crotch.

'I've never got over that fire,' he said. 'Sometimes wished I'd died in it myself. Thirty years' unpublished work, correspondence, drafts for translations, sketches for new books. Fell asleep with a fag in one hand and a Scotch in the other – how I always go to bed. But why I didn't go up myself, well, I don't know. I suppose I must be a bloody phoenix. Would be the one night without one of my little Venuses in attendance.'

White beard. White hair flowing out like foam from the globe of his head. Fingers and beard stained yellow with the nicotine. Untipped Italian cigarettes. He had one in his mouth now and chewed on it ruminatively as he spoke.

'I knew Dylan. Not the way they made him out to be in

all those books. But then academics are such wankers. Well, maybe he was that way with them, seeing as how that was what they needed. He was a chameleon, a greedy Welsh chameleon. I mean that *accent*. One had looked forward to finding out how green was his valley, small gritty chapels full of Celtic lament. When he turns up, he's Oxbridge. Lord Reith's BBC announcers. He learned that the way you and I learned Latin. Chameleon. A song and dance man. But then I suppose all writers have to set out to please someone. Graves thought it was a dominatrix called the Muse, with a whip in one hand and his balls in the other. Don't know who Eliot was trying to please. Maybe the Archbishop of Canterbury. The *TLS*. Pound. Once upon a time (God help us!) it might even have been Vivienne. Poor Vivienne. Mad as a sodding hatter and the last thing Tom needed for his entrée into English cultural life.

'Now I gather they try to make out she just had an acute case of PMT, and Tom stole all her best lines. They know nothing, you know, absolutely bugger all. Got to go for another Jimmy Riddle. Fifty-five times a day, the one time I counted. I'm a urinous sieve. I'm a fishnet stocking without even a leg inside it.'

He left the room again. The young man sipped at the whisky and soda Jeremy Carlton had mixed for him. It was at least a triple. The whisky's acid scoured the back of his throat. He looked down at the book in front of him: *The Obsequies of Ferris Miles*. On the title page Jeremy had written:

To Tim Dalgleish
A searcher after the searcher
From Pentheus the Inebriate
Don't get as torn as I've been

J.C., Firenze, 1985

Tim looked through the window. He could see the duomo over the other side of the river. It was the first time he had been to Florence, and it was the first time he had been paid to go abroad to write an article. That night, Jeremy Carlton had suggested, they should go out and have dinner together. He remembered his editor's admonition: Don't drink more than one of the drinks he mixes, and be careful where he lets you take him – you'll be paying for everything, which means that *I'll* be paying for everything.

'Do you mind if we go somewhere where the prices are reasonable?' he asked later, after taking his fourth drink from the writer.

'Well, not too reasonable, surely?' Jeremy said with a smile. 'After all, you are on expenses, aren't you? Well then.'

As they walked over the Ponte Vecchio, Jeremy talked and talked, and Tim looked about him at the buildings and the Arno. He resolved to be up early in the morning to see some of this town alone. Jeremy steered him through the streets towards his favourite restaurant. Tim checked the prices on the menu quickly. It wasn't all that expensive. Besides, a premonition told him this was the last interview the old man was ever likely to give.

They drank the Chianti and dipped spoons into the minestrone.

'Why did I leave England? Well, that's a short question, but I fear a long answer. After the war a sort of huge grey blanket came down on the place. Not during the war, mind you. I rather enjoyed London in the Blitz. There was more than one way of getting blitzed, I can tell you. And the women became . . . let's say more continental in regard to the bestowing of favours. Lots of long cold evenings during the blackout.

'But afterwards, well, I felt as though they'd have rationed the air if they could. I actually went to Africa, you know. I proposed a magazine to the British Council. They were rather keen on it at that point. I think the government wanted to be seen to be giving the chaps with black faces a sense of their own importance, culturally speaking, of course – then they might not all want their countries back at the same time. They got that one wrong, like everything else.

'Found myself actually running some sort of marriage agency. Don't ask me how. Not even sure I can remember. But I was actually quite good at it. Except I couldn't resist giving a cuddle to the ones who couldn't find husbands. Don't worry, I used to say to them, I'll marry you if none of the others will. Always found African women oddly compelling. And that's how I came to have three African wives at the same time, I certainly didn't plan it. The British

Consulate were not best pleased, I'm afraid. They thought it might be better if I visited another continent. Quickly. Even paid my fare.

'And that's how I found myself here. Very first night I arrived, I was walking across the piazza and a chap walks up with his wife and says – I had black hair in those days, I think I was probably quite a looker, from a girl's point of view – he says, *Scusi*, the way only an Englishman can say it, as though he's trying to bring a bone up out of his throat. No need for that, I said, speak the language you normally use. Do you know what he said? He turned to his wife and said, Good God, he's a Brit. Looks just like a bloody wop, doesn't he, darling? I resolved there and then never to go home to dear old blighty. And I never have. Even arranged for them to bury me here. Well, up on the hills over there, actually. This Chianti is rather good, isn't it? I'm sure that paper of yours can run to another bottle.'

By the time Tim had manoeuvred him on to the subject of his famous journal, *Nuevo*, his own memory was blurring, though Jeremy seemed to grow more precise and articulate with each drink he sank. Could anyone really start the day that many drinks down? Tim wondered. The names went flying through the air, a jumbled history of twentieth-century poetry.

'Pound's tragedy was that he felt he had to do everything. Dante didn't feel obliged to write tracts on economics, but Ezra did. He felt there was no starting point, you see. So he had to become the abecedarian of culture. He had to give modern man a hornbook to learn his letters by. And there was all of that business with fascism, though some of them do talk twaddle about it. For God's sake, there were even prominent Jews in the fascist party in Italy in those days. It wasn't like Germany.

'Now I don't know where it's going. That Frenchman they all drone on about – what's his name? – Derrida. Claims there is no presence in language, doesn't he? That all we have is a myth of presence, everything else is deferral and dispersal. Misses the point entirely. All myths turn absence into presence, and language is precisely where they do it. The very beginning of Novalis's *Pollen*: Three letters conjure the word God, one line's the revelation of a million things. That language may trace an absence most of the time does not mean the breath of presence can't cross it, like wind over a wheatfield. But the French are so morbidly analytical. Every Frenchman I've ever known can tell you exactly how many women he's had. Some of them can tell you how many times they did it, and how long it lasted as well. I sometimes wonder if they have an orgasm abacus. Descartes did most of his philosophising in bed, you know. Very French that. Simply hadn't occurred to him there was anything else you might do there.

'Well, that was nice. Really. And do thank that editor of yours too, will you? What's his name? That's right. There's a little place down along the river where you can buy me a cognac.'

When Tim woke the next day, he knew he'd never make it round the town, and when he finally made the immense journey from his bed to the wardrobe he realised he'd gone through the whole of his expenses except for ten lira. Fortunately he had his return bus ticket to the airport.

Jeremy was already deep into the bottle of Scotch by the time he arrived.

'It's the best thing, you know, if you're feeling a bit tricksy. I had my first at five this morning. Feel fine. Leaky but fine.'

Tim prevailed on him for coffee.

'I've just finished a poem. Could I read it to you, do you think? It's called "Winter Veil". You never get used to not having it, you know, take my word for it. Don't pass up any opportunities at your age because by the time you get to mine, you'll lie awake at night and wonder what it might have been like. Every woman's slightly different from all the others, even when they're twins. I can vouch for that. They don't come any more. Even the kinder signoras round here. I'd have to pay. But it's either that or the whisky, and a chap's got to be sensible.'

He read the poem. Tim couldn't follow a single word of it, but he said how fine he thought it.

Tim made it back to London and still had a headache the next day. He wrote his article, 'Jeremy Carlton and the Emigration of English Poetry', and then forgot about it. Only when it came out three months later did he remember his promise. He packed two copies carefully, together with the bags of curry powders – 'One thing Italy's hopeless for' – and posted them surface mail. Allow at least two weeks, the man at the Post Office had said. So when he read it in the Sunday papers ten days later, he could only assume Jeremy had probably never had the opportunity to read the one or taste the other.

English Poet Killed in Fire in Florence

The firemen said he must have been smoking in bed. Tim hoped that he'd at least had a glass of Scotch in his other hand, and had managed to finish it before the flames arrived.

Great White

I'd been on the train all night. No sleeper: I'd left too late to book one. The only thing about me that shone were my camera lenses. The rest was dull, grey, dusty, unshaven.

It was all down to my boss on the *Herald* – he'd got wind that the Reconcilers were to have another ceremony, and this time he wanted pictures. I'd made other arrangements and told him. The other arrangements were in the other room getting out of cotton into silk, but he wouldn't be shifted. I'd need telephoto lenses, he said, he wanted the closest shots I could get. My Other Arrangements left without a word half an hour later and I doubt she'll be back.

This was the third one we knew about, but the boss reckoned there'd been more, many more. The three had all ended in deaths – two by snake bite, one from a jaguar sprung from a zoo. He'd heard this one was going to be marine, he said.

'Marine?'

'That's what I've heard.'

'They're going to apologise to flatfish?'

'I'm just telling you what I've heard.'

I needed a drink. All night long on a train with no bed and no buffet and every time my eyes started closing my Other Arrangements went striding through me. She'd been called Alice and I was starting to feel like the looking glass. Then I'd wake up again, wipe the tears of condensation from the window and quietly mourn. I needed a drink and a strong one before this ceremony, whatever it was, started. It was now eleven and the boss's info was that it would get under way at twelve.

This wasn't much of a town. There was a main street and a couple of unmain streets and that was about it. Everything pointed to the beach and the little marina. This was a surf-and-season town. There was a bar open, a place called Sandy's. Sandy or his sidekick was standing in front of his bottles with the same look of distraction that the Manet lady has in the picture. He had a glass in one hand and a cloth in the other, but he wasn't so much cleaning the glass as performing some sort of meditation technique with it. It struck me that it would make a good shot, sort of Edward Hopper – everything here is empty, but nothing's emptier than me – but I was in a lethal mood. The boss had commissioned telephoto ceremony takes, and that was what the boss was going to get. If he wanted a portrait of a community, he could talk Cartier-Bresson out of retirement.

'A Scotch,' I said, 'a large one. Plenty of ice.' This place was already seriously hot. He gave me the kind of look cops give you when they've pulled you over for speeding.

'You a stranger?'

'Why don't we cut the John Wayne crap?' I said. 'I've just spent twelve hours on a train with no sleep and no drink, now will you kindly serve me a whisky with ice?'

'No drinks,' he said. 'Not until after the ceremony. And only if it's a success. You a reporter?'

'Photographer,' I shouted. 'I'm a photographer. Look. Here's my Leica. Here are my lenses. Here's my film. That's what I do, that's my job. Your job's serving drinks, so why don't you get on and serve one?'

'Those are the rules,' he said mildly. 'And if I were you, I wouldn't go flashing that camera around unless it's properly insured.'

He walked out. Exited stage-left, to leave shot of lone camera reporter centre-stage, leaning on bar, disconsolate. This was not shaping up to be one of my happier assignments. I left and walked down along the seafront. They were gathering there. The first thing that struck me was they were all in white, the men and women both. In this glare with that degree of reflecting surface, I'd have to compensate with the exposure. Couldn't work out what the other thing was immediately. I walked along, cursing quietly to myself. There were shops that were no more than huts with surfing gear and inflatables. Cafés and hot-dog stands, though no one seemed to be doing any business. Then I realised. Even through the noise of my temper I heard it: that silence. All these people here and nobody talking. I hadn't seen so many people in silence since Kennedy's funeral.

There was a makeshift harbour between two piers, where

a display marina had been rigged up. Dolphins, the sign at the station had said. The figures on the beach were all grouped in front of this. Some had their eyes closed, some crouched, some rocked back and forth. I found the best position I could and took out the camera. This blazing light was burning everything up. I started fitting the 200 lens. I felt a hand on my wrist. It was the lady next to me, roused from her little reverie by these lumps of black metal and glass eyes amid all that white.

'No,' she said.

Now, it's odd. Most of the places I go people don't want me to take my shots. Six months ago in East Timor they nearly shot me, but they've never stopped me. I just keep on pointing and clicking. But there's something about this scene . . . Anyway, one thing I've learned over the years is, once the action starts, they forget you're there. I'd managed to get the lens on. I could compensate exposures with my eyes shut. My fingers knew that Leica better than they knew my face, better than they were planning to get to know my Other Arrangements. Why couldn't I have specialised in glam shots like Charlie? Then I'd have got paid for having Other Arrangements, I could have had a new set sliding into position every day.

I didn't notice them getting up at first. With heat and exhaustion I'd almost gone out. Also a humming had started up, I don't know what it was, some kind of mantric murmur they were all joining in on. Anyway, it was pretty soothing, and I was very happy to be soothed for a while. But my shutter finger started twitching, it's like a war wound with the weather, and I knew some movement, some small commotion was getting ready to announce itself.

The woman herself was about fifty, a big lady, long dark hair over her shoulders dressed in a white shift and sandals. She got up behind the microphone stand at the beach end of the pier. First, she made this grand bow to the sea, the way priests used to do in front of altars, then she looked up at the sky and called out something I couldn't fathom, then she lay flat out on the pier stones with her arms outstretched. Finally she stood up again and came to within a foot of the mike.

'It is the time of reconciliation,' she said. Her eyes were closed as far as I could see, but it might just have been the glare off the water and these acres of whiteness. 'We have been asked to come forward and speak, not with our words (for who could believe them now, after what we have done?) but with our bodies. Our bodies are the one word we have which can still be believed. The Christian martyrs knew this when they gave their own flesh to fire, to water, to ice and to the jaws of the hungry creatures. Even the torturers cannot translate a body into lies. Only words lie.

'We have slashed our mother's face with our tools and our weapons, we have cut into her veins for our glory, we have slaughtered her children and eaten them, when all the time she offered us food from the trees and the fields, food which didn't bleed if you cut it, food which didn't cry out, food which didn't have faces pleading for mercy.

'We have worshipped a false god. We have worshipped

the ovens of destruction. We have worshipped speed. We fly through the air, the air that was given to birds, and we plunder whole forests so that the birds cannot live there. Our cities are ugly, our children are sick from breathing the fumes of our machines. Now it's coming to an end. The air has a hole in its head and, if we don't stop, the sun that gave life will take it away again.

'She hears us but she does not believe. Why should she? She has heard us use our man-god to lie through, she has heard us use words for our treaties, treaties which robbed every peace-loving and earth-worshipping people until we hid them away on reservations and let them rot. Those were the people she loved and she knows what our words did to them.

'She listens, though. She is always listening. And she wants us reconciled, for we are her children too. Only the words of our bodies will she swallow. Our other words are poison to her. And she speaks through her creatures. When her rage against us has ceased, their hungers will settle. It is her will, not ours.'

She fell down on to the stones again, arms outstretched, then stood up, turned around and made a beckoning gesture to the sea. Some men started up and operated a small derrick at the end of the pier, which lifted the sea gate. There were no dolphins I could make out.

I hardly noticed the younger woman until she was nearly at the bottom of the pier. She couldn't have been older than eighteen. Blonde hair halfway down her back, the same long white shift as the older lady, no sandals. At the end of the pier two more women stood and as she came between them they caught the shift by its hem and lifted it over her head in one liquid movement, as though it were part of a ceremony they'd practised. I would have liked to use my telephoto to get a closer look, but something stopped me.

The naked girl made the same beckoning gesture to the sea, then dived into the water. She splashed and kicked about in there and then the others round the edges kicked and splashed too, until the whole rim of the harbour was turning water.

There's an extraordinary grace to a shark's fin above the waves, something it conveys of the power beneath it. I suppose we're impressed by anything so suited to its element, given the way we stumble and lope about out here in the air. A cry went up from the end of the pier and everyone stopped splashing. The girl herself switched from these ungainly kicks to a perfect crawl. She was an expert swimmer.

As it came through the sea gate, the great white slowed up and I could have sworn it saw us all, took us all in. Then it circled her, once then twice as she continued her stroke. On the third circuit it suddenly swerved and thrashed. The first hit must have been in the middle and I think the bite must have been so strong it broke her back. Something snapped, I could see that from the way her head whipped back. Then it just kept turning and thrashing, shaking whole chunks of the body in its jaws. Froths of blood were flung out above the water. Within half a minute all that was left were chunks of red flesh bobbing on the harbour swell. The shark circled once and was gone.

No one had spoken. Now the two women who had disrobed her came to the pier edge and threw down her shift on to the water. During all this, I'd never once reached for my camera. The announcement lady came back out. She bowed to the sea three times, then she came back to the microphone.

'One day we shall ride on their backs as we rode once on the backs of dolphins. One day the whales will not throw themselves on our beaches to die, as they try to get a last desperate message through to us. One day the scorpion's sting will make our children well. Our bodies are the only language she will listen to.'

I booked into the one hotel. They said I could have some Scotch only if I were a resident. I poured myself two fingers, but after the first sip I put it down. Later I called the boss and told him my Leica had broken down. First time I'd ever known it happen. I'd be writing to the firm.

'Did you see it?' he said.

'Yes.'

'Could you write it up?'

'Sure,' I said, 'that's my job, isn't it?'

Later I stood by the window as the darkness started to shut down the horizon. I could hear the waves but the town stayed silent.

Logical Positivists

He tapped *Close* into the keyboard and watched as the screen started to display its shut-down routines in a concertina of multi-coloured icons. He liked this on Friday evening. It was a kind of quietus to his week's work. It was his acquittal. But it made him sad, too, like a lover waving goodbye on a train as it pulled out of the station. Of all the agencies he had to work with, the computer was the only one he regretted saying goodbye to every Friday evening.

The magazine was called *Scenes and Dreams* and it was a glorified listings rag, topped by a froth of inanity and self-importance in the centre pages. The articles this week had been 'How Aerobics Saved My Life' by a London actress whose life, in his opinion, might more usefully have been lost; 'Beauty Is the Soul's Cosmetic' by a politician who had come as close to abolishing her own soul as was possible; and 'Why I Have to Sleep with So Many Women' by one of those men still quaintly designated as stars, this one merely twinkling away now as the darkness beckoned. Jesus! He felt like apologising to the computer for contaminating it with such stuff. Still, this was his job. This was how he paid his rent. Since his philosophy degree qualified him for nothing other than teaching (an impossibility, an obscenity), he had found a corner he could function in. He was literate and could operate the machine. He would not leave unless they sacked him.

He put the plastic bag over his screen and went to get his jacket from the hook. It was a warm Friday evening in South Kensington. He said goodnight to the boss. He was free until Monday. Each week he thought to himself that he must make plans for the weekend. Contact an old friend. Arrange a trip. Somehow, though, he never did. Somehow the weekend came round again and there he was with no plans at all. He stepped round the corner as he usually did, and went into Creek's. Already the wine bar was filling up with revellers smiling their way into the weekend debauch. As usual, he picked up his half-carafe of dry white wine and made his way over to the dark corner with the little fake candle blanching the table. It was quieter there and with the lamp angled properly he had enough light to read by.

My Memories of Wittgenstein by Lady Felicity Haight was his present volume. He had worked his way halfway through it so far. What intrigued him was that the woman obviously didn't know the man at all, his favourite man, the man to whom he sometimes thought he owed his sanity. She didn't even know who he was. He saw her only when it was unavoidable to do so and then told her off for whatever it was she was getting up to. Yet this was apparently sufficient basis for her to write a book about him, and then have it published by Cambridge University Press. Anyway, the author was a diligent recorder and had dutifully written down everything the philosopher had ever said to her. These few pages made up for all the dross that surrounded them. He picked it up at page 132. He took a first long pull at the wine and it scored an impression somewhere towards the back of his head, acidulous and multi-coloured. A vinaigrette to top his salad days. A piquancy of elation followed by oblivion. This was the pattern of his weekend drinking.

She sidled over so slimly and silently that he had not registered her sitting down: Anne Holmes, the new publicity manager. She had only been there two weeks. He had been there six years. Very small, blonde, bright-eyed. Degree in English, they said. All computer operatives were graduates now. He had been polite to her – he was polite to everybody. He thought the possibilities of communication had been radically over-estimated, while politeness allowed at least for a shield both sides could employ.

'Hello,' he said, 'I'm sorry I didn't see you there. Your glass is empty, too. Have some of this.'

'How kind,' she said.

He poured some wine into her glass from his carafe.

'I'm afraid I've interrupted your reading,' she said. She had strange eyes. They stared out uneasily from her face as though they hadn't expected to land there. Blue-grey. Myopic possibly.

'It's not very good,' he said.

'May I look?'

He handed the book over to her. She flipped through the pages with that odd gesture people have, as though they were looking at the inside of a coat to check its lining.

'Looks interesting anyway,' she said. This made him cross.

'Not if you actually read the words instead of counting the pages.'

'Whoops,' she said and started to stand up. 'Only dropped by to say hello.'

'No, I'm sorry,' he said. 'My fault. It's this book, it makes me bad-tempered. This woman didn't know Wittgenstein at all. He obviously thought she was of no significance whatsoever. I think he probably tried to avoid her, as far as possible. But she pursued him with her twaddle about politics and her sentimentality about religion, and her anecdotal tiresomeness about her love life.

'He tells her the politics is a self-delusion. With all her right thinking about Spain and Nazism and what-have-you, she achieves nothing of any value for anyone. Her religiosity he detests because it has none of the dignity of the ancient customs of belief he admired, and all the clamorousness of the daily newspapers he detested. As for her love affairs, she evidently can still not understand that what she thought of as her freedom, he considered her enslavement. And what she imagined was her flouting of convention was to him merely the fulfilment of the tritest conventions of her time.'

She looked at him in the murk of the back corner and smiled.

'Sounds like a floozy out of her depth to me.'

'Yes,' he said, starting to smile too. 'Precisely. An upper-class floozy out of her depth, to make matters even worse.'

'What a twat,' she said and he laughed. 'Why are you reading it then, if it's so bloody awful?'

'I read anything about Wittgenstein,' he said. 'I revere the man.'

'Why?'

'He explained what you cannot say. Many of the problems in life come from people trying to say the unsayable. By learning what's impossible to say, you avoid trying to feel things it's impossible to feel.'

'Let me get you another glass of wine,' she said. 'Your carafe's finished now.'

She came back with a bottle. He had already started to like her.

'My problem's not having impossible feelings,' she said. 'I usually have entirely possible feelings, but always for entirely impossible people.'

The bar was filling up. All the local offices and shops and banks were setting their alarms and closing the doors on their valued employees. The bar would be full for an hour, and then they would start to leave for the country, or wherever it was they all went. He often found himself there at the end when the others had gone. He did need a friend, even he knew that. It had been a long time. His flat in Notting Hill had grown lonely. Jacqueline.

'Whereof one cannot speak, thereof one must be silent,'

he said, smiling at her. He seldom smiled. 'Wovon Mann nicht sprechen kann darüber muss Mann schweigen.'

'That's interesting,' she said. 'What's that from?'

'The *Tractatus Logico-Philosophicus*.'

Her smile seemed to him now a mixture of bewilderment and frank invitation. He filled up both their glasses.

'It was the first stage of his philosophy,' he said. 'It put forward what's been called the picture theory of language. You can find in any proposition a resemblance between what's going on in the proposition and the way of things in the world.'

'I don't understand,' she said.

'Well, let's take a simple statement,' he said. 'I drink this glass of wine. Now *this glass of wine* refers to something here on the table. *I* refers to the subject of the action and *drink* here is a copula – the activity bringing the two things together.'

'Is that the same as copulate?' she said.

'They share the same root. Bringing together. You could state it in more abstract terms of the sort that Wittgenstein frequently shied away from. You could say you see a subject here. Before him is the object of his need.'

'So you only have to put a copula between them,' she said.

'The dynamic force that the copula represents takes away anything that could truly come between them,' he said. She wore a single milky pearl hanging from a gold chain round her neck. Her neck was so thin. He was counting the veins. He wondered if the veins on her breasts stood out like that.

'Do you enjoy your work?' she said.

'It's work. Pays the rent, keeps this particular form of life functioning. Fortunately I can work with the computer mostly.'

'You prefer that?'

'Yes. It allows for a certain clarity of expression.'

'Whereas people don't?'

'With them it can often be harder.'

'Or softer,' she said.

He had no right to his anger when her boyfriend arrived to collect her, he knew that. But the way her face uncreased with joy at the sight of this grinning creature called Henry saddened him immeasurably.

'Do finish the bottle,' she said. 'And see you Monday.'

He left the bottle half-full and set off walking towards Notting Hill by way of High Street Kensington. He kept thinking he might call in at one of the many restaurants he passed. He'd been to most of them at one time or another. He'd think about food later.

Of course, Wittgenstein came to abandon the picture theory. In his later philosophy he looked on language as being analogous to the use of tools. A word meant whatever we used it to mean within the given rules of its environment. This had one consequence though which he was not sure Wittgenstein had foreseen: if the environment should be one of relentless destructiveness and a word like love were to be used in that environment to signify manipulation, untruth, blackmail and deceit, then within the terms of the language game in which it was used, that is what the word would come to mean. Jacqueline.

He saw Gerry's ahead of him. Surely he would not go in there? It was loud and unpleasant, it played music he detested and the drinks were expensive. Also it happened to be owned by Gerry Knowles, whom he'd first met in the little sandwich shop Gerry used to manage round the corner from the office in South Kensington. In the six years that he had been sitting before his computer screen, Gerry had been busy. These days he drove a Bentley, or usually had it driven for him. Gerry's was also filled with women every Friday night. He went in.

There was just enough of his mind left to think in, the rest was sagged with the music; but if Wittgenstein could stay in his observation post on the Eastern Front all night, as the shells flew around him, and still compose his thoughts for the *Tractatus*, surely he could survive this.

He leaned over the book at the far end of the bar, clutching his drink. Lady Felicity Haight was explaining how she thought Wittgenstein's sexual repression was responsible for the ferocity he showed in the face of logical error. The book slammed shut on his fingers.

'Hello, mate,' Gerry shouted above the smoky swamp of sound. 'Still philosophising, are you? You should be getting philosophical with some of those girls over at the edge of the dance floor. The one in the orange skirt told me last night she had that Bertrand Russell in the back of the cab once.'

'Wouldn't have thought she was old enough,' he said, but Gerry was already off down the bar again, scissors in hand. His party trick at weekends was to cut in half the ties of pinstriped businessmen, frisky solicitors, or even Members of Parliament out looking for a bit of rough. They all seemed to approve of Gerry. A barrow boy in his own Bentley showed what a great country it really was.

He left, as he always did, after the first drink. As he walked up Kensington Church Street he decided he had better eat something. He went into the Greek Café. He ordered a kebab and a glass of red wine. He opened the book again.

Lady Felicity was explaining that Wittgenstein's inability to acknowledge what he most wanted meant that sin and madness both became one realm for him, the realm of error. A mistake here was a catastrophe. He closed the book, shut one eye and looked at that confident smile on the cover. He tipped his wine glass over gently till the red wine spilt down the side of it and gathered at the base. Then he pressed the glass down hard on that face and turned it round. When he lifted it again Lady Felicity had been branded for ever.

'Oh, now look at that,' the Greek said, come to collect the empty plate.

'It's a Vienna circle,' he said.

'That's a cake isn't it?'

'No,' he said, 'no, you're thinking of a Vienna slice. Wittgenstein himself was never a logical positivist, you know. They were so pleased at how little you could truthfully say in language, but it terrified him.'

'Another book of philosophy then?' the Greek said.

'Yes.'

'We invented it you know. Our boys thought it up.'

When he got back to the flat, it was all quiet. It was summer so there was not even a whimper of complaint from the central-heating system. He had disappointed this flat and he knew it. He had taken it on false pretences. The flat had always dreamt of children dancing on its carpeted back, their thin voices rising up out of its darkness to make the lights in its little sky shine. But the flat didn't complain any more. It didn't want anything else getting broken.

He sat down at the table. The photograph of Wittgenstein stared manically out at him. On the shelf behind was the little row of icons. He walked over to the one which had Jacqueline's face framed in it. Now they said she was even having a child, with the man she called her Henry. He turned the picture face downwards.

In the morning he woke to the white silence of the ceiling, the knotted inconsequence of his bedsheets, the soiled lament of the used clothes in the corner. He lay flat on his back for two minutes, then he said, 'The limits of my language are the limits of my world.' How many problems in philosophy or belief were really no more than a knot in language, a logical entanglement? Unthread that knot and the problem disappeared. After a few more minutes he said, 'Superstition is the belief in the causal nexus.' Then he shouted, 'Der Glaube an den Kausalnexus ist der Aberglaube.'

The flat said nothing, for the moment. But then the flat had its own language and its own rules, and he knew that.

Rembrandt Dying

As in the land of darkness, yet in light.
Samson Agonistes

So often I showed the gleam inside its black surrounds. So often the words of John filled my mouth: And the light shineth in darkness; and the darkness comprehended it not. The darkness swallowed Saskia and Hendrickje, and last year even my beloved Titus. I lie here and wait as it starts at last to make a meal of me as well.

Light and dark: both incalculable. No man can trace the tracks of those bitumen veins back to divinity. In the house of Menasseh ben Israel I met Spinoza once, that pale, long-faced Jewish angel, counting up how many zeroes could disappear into the godhead before it finally exploded. Scripture disappointed him, deficient as it was in mathematic demonstration. And how much of my own money disappeared, treating the world as a matter for calculus in the markets of the East Indies, trading days and years as though the paradise they longed for was the inside of a luminous equation? (But the face of a Jew is a map of time. The face of a Jew is the word of God, wrinkling fondly in history's weather.)

Saskia had the laughing beauty of a moneyed child, though she did not laugh much towards the end, sick, sad and sweating in her bed, waiting for another child to show its bloody face between her legs. She gave me Titus and then slipped back silently into the dark. Strange how her dowry oppressed me, made me even more reckless in my purchases than I had been before: the accoutrements of kings – prints, busts and helmets bid for by the richest collectors travelling the world. But I outbid them all and put my new possessions on to canvases. Over and over again I painted Samson and Delilah, the smiling woman to whom the man yields his secret and his strength. Blindness. Imagine that, your own small world of dark even before the big one of the grave descends. Do women make us blind? Can the love of them cost a man his eyes? Aristotle staring at Homer's bust, that sightless little world of the imagination no philosopher's light can hold a candle to. And Tobit raging at Anna, sightless until his son lays fingers on his lids and lets him see again. Save us from the righteousness of those too old to sin. Let our children redeem us with their touch.

Some of my most joyous paintings I made after Saskia's death. A strange exhilaration comes when someone that you love has dropped into the grave. You look about you later, and see how bright the sunlight is, how ludicrous and wild is the yellow in the egg's yolk, how rich the taste of even the cheapest wine as your tongue curls round it. You are still alive, wombing your little miracle, even though death's bat wing clipped your ear. And Titus was so beautiful, his little face riddled in perplexity at the small conundrums that we put before him.

Celibacy is hard even for a Nazarite, and I was never that – though Samson was, and much good it did him. I've never kept myself separate from any good the world afforded. I painted myself as Paul, but did I ever have his passion for the judgment of the living? Could I ever see my wounds as qualifying me so readily for heaven? Disease and disquiet were that man's bar mitzvah, but God gave me his glory in candlelight, and between the sheets, in wedlock or out of it. Saskia's shadow had deepened the dark around my portraits, even while their faces smiled and told the world to do its worst. Hendrickje's face around the door, that little beckoning moon in my evening sky. She raised her shift to show me her strong thighs. My fingers, grained with paint and printer's ink, found her breasts and gave thanks for such softness. How paint that? Mennonite: only forgiveness and humility count in the eyes of the Lord. All the rest is merely decoration for the mind of man.

Some Christians thought otherwise. The Amsterdam Church Council: Hendrickje Stoffels lives as a whore with Rembrandt, the painter. The whoredom wasn't in our house but in their hearts, those who threatened to exclude her from the communion of Jesus Christ. (Can any man on earth do that? Who is he? And how dare he? Throwing first stones after his own desires.) Hendrickje with a child already in her womb, listening to their anathemas, spoken in such measured tones, the gravity of the reformed tongue. And Spinoza, still beading the Almighty's attributes across an abacus, received a mighty admonition from his brethren too: Cursed be he by day and cursed be he by night; cursed be he when he lies down and cursed be he when he rises up; cursed be he when he goes out and cursed be he when he comes in. The Lord will not pardon him: the anger and wrath of the Lord will rage against him and will bring upon him all the curses which are written in the Books of the Law. *Ecce homo*: behold the man I bring before you here this day for condemnation. Start sharpening now the implements of his passion, beginning with your own metallic tongues. Let the burin and the graver cut commandments in the dead flesh of your mouths.

My face was always life's clock and I painted the hours moving as the hands crawled round. Saw my own flesh inscribe my own mortality. From my first etchings I portrayed the outlines of death, the black lines that give form to the blankness and vacuity of the unstained sheet. Even my angels had mottled faces as the little veins of red exploded on the brush, one flesh with the slaughtered ox, my axed and skewered brother. How we crucify the world each day. Saskia is Flora, burdened with the world's fecundity, and Hendrickje steps on still as life itself, though she is dead, standing in those flowing waters, raising the folds of her shift as though it were a chalice, lifted up in sacrifice and thanks. I painted her as Danaë, her round body welcoming the gold of Zeus. Not cash, but love's amber swiftly melting. The classical: so much geometric beauty I never did see in Leiden or Amsterdam. Why lie for symmetry's sake? Flesh is lopsided and warm: it is only the skeleton which balances so easily on the walls of those anatomy rooms. Jesus died a criminal's death, as did those whom Tulp laid out to dig his knife through while Amsterdam applauded.

Titus is the angel leaning over my shoulder now, as I showed him leaning once over Matthew's, the smiling whisper of his face from beyond the shadow. I have portrayed myself as everything from a demon howling its curse out of the grimoire, to the apostle in prison awaiting his redemption. But notice always how the face stares out into the dark, stares into that vast and baffling curtain always falling.

In my nativities the light shone from the infant, burning brighter than a church full of candles, however white its walls. Little bundle in the crib that couldn't even speak a word. But the dark stays solid always. One thing no room ever loses. And when at last it positions us thus or thus, in a final gesture, we stay still and wait until it finishes the portrait. We don't move, not even to take a spoonful of air into our lungs, until the portrait is finished.

Cult

Thomas Treely. The last day.

I write this in the hours remaining. This brief explanation of my life and work must be complete before the evening's ceremonies, though I am doubtful it could help anyone towards the path, even assuming the authorities do not destroy all documents relating to my teaching.

What is a life? Do you imagine it can be set down in these words, laid out in these little coffins spaced so neatly across the page? Husks and traces, the chrysalis sheath where the pupa once grubbed. I shall put down whatever words are delivered to me.

Of my childhood what is there to say? A psychotherapist I once consulted, in the days before my enlightenment, said I was unusually formed in that both my parents constituted law, neither of them an escape from the law. My father shouted the law and my mother whimpered and whined it. Ground between the two of them, my little mind learned one thing: history offers no escape. If you need a tunnel, you'll have to dig it for yourself.

Roman Catholicism. They preached love but they didn't

mean it. They preached joy and they didn't mean that either. They were as joyless and unloving as everyone else, and with hell the likely outcome of so many of their lives, they had a unique tract of melancholic misery all their own. My first understanding came: Jesus made people free, but now his followers wanted to imprison me in his shadow. They called one part of the shadow church and another morality, but it was all dark and cold and gave no comfort.

I was fat and small for my age. The accident when I was five meant that I was half-blind too. I couldn't run more than a few yards without being out of breath. Everyone held me in contempt – boys and girls. They knew I was clever, though. In fact, I was even cleverer than they thought.

At Oxford I became a Marxist. This seemed a more interesting manoeuvre of the mind than any of the others on offer, and gave me at least a first glimpse of millennial expectation, seeing the shape of time. The problem was nihilism: too many of them only believed in disbelief. They were handsome too. I did not have that distraction. Now my hair fell out. Small fat blind bald.

Much of it was a language of despair. These people ached with exasperation at the tawdry gimmickry that surrounded them, and the lacklustre turnip-heads who held sway in the world. But they didn't really believe, they only disbelieved. That makes you weak. Underneath all the disbelief, what belief was left?

I studied English and started to notice an odd thing: how people put aside with a smile whatever is most disconcerting to them. The supernatural in Shakespeare is a case in point. A man does not devote huge amounts of intellectual energy to anything which is unimportant to him. Shakespeare gazed at the uncanny for a long time. I brought this up with my smiling tutor. He sent me to Freud to clean out the stable of my mind. So I read Freud on 'The Uncanny', and found his obsession with demonology and possession something insufficiently remarked upon. I showed some of the darker passages to my tutor. He threw his head back and laughed. He threw back his beautiful golden head and laughed.

I studied, though, for my mind was capable of sharper thought than the minds of those sent to teach me. I knew this because I knew the nature of the world I lived in: the age of monsters, the age of Hitler, Stalin, Pol Pot, nuclear bombs and chemical warfare. Nuremberg for the Germans but early release for Lieutenant Calley of the My Lai Massacre. While my tutor shook his golden tresses like a god out of Homer, the most materialistic society in the world's history was devoting many of its finest minds to parapsychology and telekinesis. The Soviet scientists were also pondering the terrible end of the planet Phaeton, and the cosmonauts so accurately portrayed by the Honshu figurines.

I had lost my faith in the apostolic succession when I came to Pope John XII — he was the tenth-century Satanist with a penchant for incest, who died moaning wildly in the act of coitus. Somehow the exact nature of the laying on of hands ceased to be of interest to me after that. I lost my faith in Marxism when I saw that it was another Pharisaism, corroding into the institutions of law what had once been a blast from the spirit. So what was to become of me now? Where could I go to leave my disbelief behind?

I would like to record my debt here to Sally Shoreham, who led me from the dusky murk into the true darkness, where I found the light. One day, in a little café in St Giles, I was looking through a book of Goya's paintings. The colossus, the courtyard with lunatics, and those witches hovering in the air and gathering for the sabbat. She looked over my shoulder for a moment, then said, 'Well?'

'I don't think it's a satire,' I said, as though I were being addressed by my tutor with the golden tresses.

'He might have intended it to be,' she said, 'but his imagination knew better than his conscious mind.' Sally invited me back to her flat. I should say that where I was brought up, the likes of Sally Shoreham were seldom seen and when they were, they were intended for someone else, not you. She was small and slim with long, straight, blonde hair and blue eyes. She was trim and gleaming. She had been bred to inherit. When we arrived at her flat, I went into her bathroom and looked in the mirror. There was nothing to be done, though. Small bald fat blind.

'What is it about yourself?' she asked gently.

'Everything.'

She started to explain, and it made sense to me. She told me in effect that the dwarf in the mirror with the ugly face and hands was the manifestation of my shrunken soul, and that my soul was shrunken because of the religion of self-hatred and self-degradation I had been raised in.

'Your will has been crippled. That's why you're ugly. Free your will and you'll be beautiful.'

'Beautiful enough for you to want me?'

'I can already see enough of the beauty in you to want you now.'

Sally's perceptions were in some ways rudimentary, and certainly the ceremonies of initiation and reversal which she put me through would seem laughably primitive to any of my own devotees, but she started me on the path. She taught me that anything which hinders will is evil; that will and intelligence are the only realities and always have been. She also made me briefly beautiful, and so gave me a taste of what was to come. She was, I suppose, a minor Crowleyite and her sex magic, while infantile, was enough to produce that sheen of silver on her skin so often noted in female adepts. And in the mirror of her flesh that night I saw my own soul. What a vision. Of course she was cold inside. That thrill of cold. The glacial mons. She was elsewhere. She uncovered the snow of her flesh and my tongue was ice in a wet cave.

It is a shame that she betrayed me and so plunged me back into a brief sojourn of ugliness and self-loathing. That showed a lack of perception on her part about the importance of my mission. A lack of perception which, as you know if you are reading this at all, cost her dear. This is not a game.

It became necessary to make a study of history. Why? Because it is said of paradise that the violent take it by force. That is said in scripture. And how can one live a life that is celebrated in scripture? Live near to one who's writing it, that's all. Stay with me.

I noted that while the men in the Marxist–Leninist Archive inside the Kremlin struggled for the correct terminology to describe the great victory in terms of the dialectics of history, Stalin himself arranged for the internal organs of the vegetarian Hitler to be shipped back from Berlin to Moscow, so he could cook and eat them. He thereby sought to ensure that any residual genius should not be wasted in the dusty earth, but might accrue instead within himself. The valley below has grown busy, and since this is the last time I'll see it while enfleshed in this compromise meat, I am going out to collect some mind-prints to take with me.

The quaint figures of commerce and fidelity have already struggled out of the dark. How I envy their separation of the dimensions, the ease with which they whistle and switch their headlights on and off. How sure they are of the road beneath them. For myself, the first time I ever looked into a mirror which stared back at me with anything other than static disbelief was when I saw those Francis Bacon paintings. In those faces I saw how space spills over into time, flowing across the canvas. The eyes and mouths smear, their expressions already escaping the space tyranny of Euclid. Icons leaking into time. The filament that separates external duration from inner time has broken down.

I go and stand before the mirror. I am undoubtedly taller, and now strikingly beautiful. The baldness which was once a negativity, an embarrassment of absence, is now my monastic crown. I have been shorn free of the age's illusions. I am wrapped in an envelope of light wherever I go.

It was of course absurd for Crowley to claim to be the Beast, assigning the number 666 to himself. He did not even understand the number's significance, though it is simple enough. It represents the combination of the actuality of the figure with its tripartite expression. So simply take the figure and multiply it by three and what do you have? 1998. This year. The year of incompletion. This year the abolitions must take place and I am here to assist them, and to make my momentous journey. The violent will take it by force.

Sally's acts of precognition greatly helped me along my journey. (Tomorrow Sally and I will be reunited, with thrones set up in the same kingdom. Not that she could have held the ritual of her departure against me. And even if she did then, she certainly wouldn't now.) If she could deliver these segments of the future to me before we had arrived there, what did this mean? Where did this leave time's mechanism? If there is an escape through time's riddles, then time is imprisonment, but the prison is no longer monolithic. So in this last phase I have stayed in time as one might rest in a hotel. Today I shall depart. Or rather, today we shall depart.

First you must coax them out of flat time and transparent

space. First you must tell them a story and riddle it with arcane lights. You must spray the leaves with a scent of gnosis and then hide a letter in a garden. Thus do they learn to unplug themselves from homogeneous time, and start at last to seek.

Then you must show them the wounds in the song, so they can hear the whimpering voices of historiography, see the slivers of bodies drowning in philology.

Take their sex away from them entirely. They only slouch in it like rented furniture. If necessary, use it yourself. That is a prophet's privilege.

Frighten them enough to start reading.

Then start to write the book they've started reading. Help them towards the title page, since they must always start at the end and work backwards.

These have been my precepts – unexceptional enough in the crescent curves of the arcana, to be sure. I advertised a little at one time. Notices on the London Underground, classified ads in the *Highbury Gazette*, coloured cards handwritten in the local stationer's. This was all futile. How can they read their way to you before you have taught them to read? You have to tempt them first across the abyss of their own incomprehension. And as they fall to their deaths, they'll find their wings.

I should perhaps talk a little about those who have been given to me. They arrived at this speed or that, according to the gravity of their failures. For some their failure was merely the success of their parents in accommodating themselves to a world where mendacity thrives. Such a great hatred stuttered inside them. What they needed, of course, was to learn how to destroy everything inside them that they held in contempt. Then they would be free and filled with light, the true light that's born in the darkness. Some were simply deficient in power. Elizabeth Crew for example, who called her problem depression, and spent time and money on endless Freudian cures for it. But her problem was not depression. It was simply that the manipulative untruths with which she attempted to control people were not very effective. Once a long time back someone had hurt her by not loving her as much as she required, so she had sworn vengeance. She was simply not very good at obtaining it. I helped her there, by introducing her to the power she needed. She even became one of my flesh companions for a while. She was however too fidgety inside her skin to hold that position for long. She wept. I could even sense her calling upon the power to imprison me. I scorched her mind, and since then she has been escorted at all times by one of the sisters.

All of my children had to learn God's vulnerability in the light of our choices. If my study of history has taught me anything, it is the absence of providence. If there ever had been a providential scheme, God has absconded from it. I remember my mother once praying that my father should receive a bonus. What a strange God she spoke to, who allowed children to shriek and die in the shower rooms of the death camps, while He did nothing, but would still intervene to enable her to buy a new sofa.

If God is vulnerable to our choices, then which choices do we wish to make? We wish to control our fate, that's all, each and every one of us. Anyone who says he doesn't is a liar. Even the holy man fasting up in the mountains, what is he doing if not dominating his own desire, teaching his body to wait upon his will? So first I teach them how to achieve their desires, then I show them how petty those desires are. I introduce them to real desire: to help put an end to time. To leave this mess of meat and shadows finally behind us.

First, though, we reverse the ceremonies that have entrapped them. We reverse their baptisms and communions and all the vows of bad faith and restriction. This can take some days. They must walk backwards through the cavern of their own initiations, widdershins round the sundial of their lives. Then they start to sense it — the field of electrical discharge all around them, their haloes of power and choice. They sense their power long before they understand anything of it. Magic. Alchemy. Kabbalah. These are words. At the centre is a power no word ever touches.

I have to stop them thinking, for thinking is Blake's Devourer swallowing the Prolific. The stone tablets of the law are nothing but desire that has petrified in the face of its freedom. My ritual of bodies has been useful here, for it takes all thought into the flesh. There have been casualties, of course, particularly in the early experimental phase. We will see them tomorrow. But no undue force was used. Meat in any case is expendable. It is the spirit alone that continues.

It is late in the afternoon. I have walked about the garden and looked across the valley. This is a most beautiful place, acquired for me by my disciples. Over the lintel stand the firesnake and the dragon. Flickering tongues. And my sigil from the grimoire. Buried with the foundations are some of the bones.

'What is the dragon?' my children asked me at first.

'Intelligence unfettered by the scruple of dead law,' I told them. 'Honest hunger. All that raves and yearns beneath the piety.'

In their new freedom, I would send them out around the local towns to exercise the power they now had access to. This they did with great success, bringing me many of my younger devotees. Bringing now it seems also the attention of the authorities – authorities with no authority at all except their prisons. No one is locked in here, in my little kingdom. This world, though, is not ours. The time has come to travel on.

I have walked about the village. They are polite, but they look at me oddly. Of course, some of their children have become my children, but I doubt they are able to consider the reasons why. Some even smile uneasily. They would like, I suspect, to lay hands upon me, but they won't do that. They see something in my eyes. I have brought so much power out of so many that I am surrounded now by a force field which is only penetrable by those I wish to admit. I know which ones have spoken while the police wrote down their words. I see them lower their eyes.

On my return I arrange the table and lay out the glasses. We have bottles of fine Margaux and, for the children, lemonade. The cyanide itself I shall mix in later, when all the preparations have been completed. I shall go and stand out in the garden in the dusk with a glass of this wine in my hand and wait for my fellow voyagers to come and join me.

I look out over the lights, lights far from this valley, the sacred lights. Those powers never slept, you see – they only dozed fitfully while waiting once more to be summoned. For how long was Hebrew no more than an intermittent flicker of prayer before the scattered scrolls? Now, in its intensity of revival across a whole country, it has awoken all the old powers. The gods of Canaan are climbing out of their wood and stone, and uncreasing their leathery faces in the sunlight. Up there too, see that light bright as a star making its way from west to east across the sky. Our transport, most likely.

And here they come now up the hill towards me, the men and women and children, with their Volvos and Saabs parked in the valley below. See how they glow with little lamps, like Samuel Palmer's congregation swaying up through the valley, making their way at last to the promised rest.

The Eating of the Shadow

A redactor? Well, who isn't one?
Part of the price you have to pay
To stand mid-way
Between a man's shadow and the sun.

In Ephesus around the year 200 there lived a man named Aliochus. He was part of the remains of that little community of the disciple John, which had once flourished there and now flourished no longer. In his youth Aliochus had dedicated himself to being a eunuch for the kingdom. He would not touch either the flesh of women or strong wine. He believed along with many of his brethren that time was reaching its belated conclusion. The focus of his attention was the Second Coming.

The little flock of John believed all the words of what we now call the Book of Revelation, the apocalypse revealed to the apostle on the island of Patmos while he was exiled there. And because of the words, 'And they shall see his face; and his name shall be in their foreheads', all of the members of this little community had the tiniest tattoo in the centre of their foreheads bearing the mark of the ChiRho.

Aliochus did not succeed in becoming sexless for Christ, and rather than be tormented in this world or possibly damned in the next, he married. As the years passed, his wife grew more proficient in the language, along with his children, and it sometimes seemed to him that there was no silence left in the world. He felt as though his mind were being nibbled away by rats. He grew confused and he took to drinking strong wine to lessen the pain of his confusion. The wine lessened the pain, to be sure, but only added to the confusion. The ascetic youth was now a stout and melancholy man.

Aliochus made a living by teaching at the little Christian academy, and because he taught grammar he had come to understand that the way a person uses language is the signature of that person's soul. So it had come to puzzle him that the signature of John's gospel and his letters was so entirely different from the signature of Revelation. The language of the latter was crude and unfashioned, that of the former polished and refined. He knew the two could not have come from the same hand.

A number of possibilities occurred to him. John on Patmos might have dictated his vision to a less literate accomplice. Yet here was a presentation of the last things and the coming of the kingdom, the most important message still to be given to the world. Surely it would have at least merited the apostle's correction, even if he had originally dictated it? What else, after all, had he to do on Patmos? Then a curious thought struck Aliochus. He had once heard a holy man in the next village say that when the true vision arrives, a man will throw away his books and burn his papers and never write another word, but only warm himself continually by the divine flames and dream of the final union. What if John had been so filled with his vision that he had merely spoken of what he had seen and heard, and one of the islanders with some rudimentary writing skills had then written some of it down, so that more than the wind should inherit it?

Aliochus wondered how accurate this process might be. He decided on a little experiment. Once he had known whole sections of the gospellers' stories and could recite them at will. But that part of his mind had fallen dull over the last few years. As the coming of the kingdom receded, his delight in gospels and creeds had diminished. Now he would set himself the task of redaction without the aid of books or conversation. In this way he hoped to discover how much truth from John's vision might have survived into the written Revelation.

His wife, who had grown plump too, sat below in the kitchen and shook her dark head. When he had converted her to the new religion, before their marriage, she had thought he was at least a sensible fellow, who would achieve some distinction in their little world, but now she realised that her mother had been right: the old lady had seen the frenzy in his eyes that the bride had missed. Her mother did not like the Christians – they hate what they love, she said, that's why they carry around the pictures of the man being tortured on the cross. Now even her daughter could see that Aliochus was locked in a small dark room with a tiny flame he could share with nobody. She only hoped he would continue to bring home the money with which to feed the children. He would come down from time to time for a beaker of wine. He said nothing to her. His children looked upon him as an oddity with which their young lives had been mysteriously burdened.

Upstairs he scraped away over his parchment and would sometimes continue by the table in moonlight. His wife slept in the other room. At first he had been horrified how little he could recall exactly. He had been so sure it was all there verbatim in his mind. But it had disintegrated like scrolls in a damp cellar, something else for the rats to eat. Then day by day this absence of exact memory facilitated something else he didn't know the name of, some force that rose to fill the holes between his quotations. It seemed to him now that he was no longer writing out the remains of a gospel which time had torn ragged with gaps. Instead he was writing his own. The gaps were now the parts he looked forward to, and he would grow annoyed if sufficient text from the original still lodged in his memory not to allow him this freedom.

With his memories of the annunciation from Luke, strange things happened. It was a god who came to make the announcement, not an angel, and Aliochus added a gloss explaining that, with the coming of the Saviour, the old gods became servants of the new. And in the account of the finding of the Christ child in the temple, Joseph and Mary left the boy behind deliberately because they were so startled by the authority of his speech at home that they thought his mission must have begun. He fled from the temple when he realised he was lonely, and if he was lonely then the Father had not yet filled up all the gaps inside him. Only when the Father's love filled each hiatus could his mission start.

Aliochus's account of the baptism of Jesus by John would have passed for orthodoxy, but when he came to the temptation in the desert, he had the most powerful urge to fill a gap, a gap that did not even exist for anyone but himself. His wife was glad to see him pack his bags and go, for she was sick of the sight of his moon-dusted face. The pilgrimage might do him some good and her mother could at last come to the house again.

Aliochus travelled by sea and land until he came to the hill in Judaea where local legend had it that Jesus had been tempted. He climbed to the top of this hill, sat down and closed his eyes. He did not pray, for he had stopped doing that. One of the little flock had once said that every word we utter is a prayer. His gospel now was his prayer. Any other formulation fell dead from his mouth.

After a few moments a guide arrived, wrapped in a grey robe. He stood before Aliochus silently, then sat by his feet. When Aliochus opened his eyes he saw the man, a thin man whose grey beard made him look older than his years.

'You need a guide,' the man said.

'A guide to what?'

'A guide to the temptation. I am the best one.'

Aliochus had travelled a long way at some expense to be here today, so he felt he could turn down no offer of enlightenment, even though it might turn out to be spurious. The guide agreed strange terms with him: that after the hours they spent together, Aliochus should give him whatever he saw fit. Then, as they walked in circles down the hill, the guide began to talk.

'Rid your mind for today at least of the usual redactions and I will give you the most authentic account of the events that happened here, which we guides have preserved among us.

'First, you might want to dispense with the term *temptation*, which was no part of the original events, and replace it with the word *suggestion*. Jesus, you may remember, was hungry, and in what has come to be known as the first temptation the one they now call the devil said, *Command this stone that it be made bread.*'

Here the guide lifted up a stone from the ones at their feet and said, 'You must be hungry too, after your long journey. Would you like some bread to eat?'

Aliochus smiled and nodded. The guide dropped the stone into the folds of his robe and seconds later pulled out a loaf, which he gave to Aliochus. 'Eat it,' he said, and Aliochus did.

'Why shouldn't stones be loaves, if the power exists and mouths are hungry? There is no shortage of stones about us, but a man can die for lack of bread. Would it be a sin to feed them because a few scorpions might lose their homes?'

They trod their spiral track in silence. Now they were heading back up the mountain. At the top the guide resumed.

'What has been written as the second temptation, which we guides call the second suggestion, was the devil's proposition that he should now hand over all this to Jesus.'

The guide swept his hand out before the face of Aliochus and suddenly the visitor saw towns and towers beneath him that he'd not noticed on his first climb to the summit.

'The mist is clearing,' the guide said. 'If Jesus had only accepted this suggestion immediately, imagine what a different gospel you could write. All the kingdoms of this world put into the hands of the Son of God. The gold on the walls of the basilica would shine with the real presence. But then perhaps they do already – we shall see.'

They started to walk down the mountain again and the guide gave Aliochus a wine skin to drink from. When they came back to the top for the last time, the guide pointed and said, 'On a clear day like this you can even see Jerusalem from here. Look.'

Aliochus looked down and there beneath him was the holy city.

'The third suggestion was that Jesus should throw himself from here, so that the angels who adored him might bear him up with their hands. It is hard now to see how this suggestion was any more reprehensible than the others. It would have given the angels great pleasure and shown an unmistakable sign to the people. And it would have provided entertainment of a divine kind, instead of the profanities so prevalent in the cities these days.

'Later, of course, Jesus did cast himself down through his own choice, into hell. And the angels did bear him up again into heaven. So the two realms, you see, were reconciled. But it could all have happened sooner on this mountain – the reconciliation of the realms. For now that reconciliation has been effected, though many of the theologians say it hasn't. Still, from time to time they give themselves away: Now is no more sin, they say, and that much at least is true.

'It is the tradition of the dead, those who would not rise again, that gives you, in the gospels you read, the words temptation, devil and hell. Where the words should be suggestion, messenger and shadow.'

Aliochus noticed something suddenly. The guide smiled.

'No, I have no shadow,' he said. 'I have eaten it and now I and my shadow are one. Do thou likewise.'

Aliochus was so grateful for the guide's information that he told him he would pay him anything he requested.

'Anything?' the guide asked.

'Anything I am able to give,' Aliochus said.

'Then send me your gospel, written in your own hand, when it is complete.'

Aliochus agreed, and after accepting some more bread and some wine from the wine skin, he left and started his long journey home.

When he arrived at his house he found that his wife's mother had moved into his room. He disapproved of his wife's mother because she hung on to the old gods. She disapproved of him because he didn't. He told his wife to take her mother back to her own home, which he knew would take some days. Then, having gone to the market and filled the deeper pots with wine, he started to write.

For three days and three nights he wrote until his gospel was complete. By the time he had finished it, he knew he could never return to the school. He knew which word they would use about his teachings, were he to propound them, but he also knew that he could not remain silent. He collected all his money from the different places where he had hidden it. Then he asked his eldest and most trustworthy son to sit next to him in the shade. He explained that he was going away on a mission for which God had appointed him. He might be some years. He explained where he had put the money, which the boy was to give to his mother on her return. He also gave him this letter for her:

My dear wife,
  I converted you to the true faith.
  Now I have more truth to add and am called away to preach it.
  Study each night with our sons my gospel.
  Barbus will read it to you.

Then last of all he gave the boy his scroll, knowing that his knowledge of Greek and his hand were good. He told the boy to copy word for word the gospel he had written, and to send the original to the address the guide had given him in Jerusalem, for he had made a solemn promise that it would arrive. Then he left. As he walked down the road from the village he saw the boy's face before him. He had the eyes of his mother when he had first seen her. The glimpse of a wild animal in the mouth of a cave. How he had wanted that animal then. He had tamed the animal, and taught it to speak his language and to kneel before his God. Now the cave was all light, but the fire in the eyes had died.

He did not need a copy of the gospel for himself, since he knew every word. Writing it had furrowed the lines through his mind.

His mission took him along the southern coast of the Black Sea. He preached the end of opposition, the marriage of black and white. He preached the eating of the shadow. He taught that the crucifixion was the last bitter moment of the conflict between the kingdoms, and that with resurrection and pentecost the two were now one. His doctrine was heard as redemption by some, as sacrilege by others. If one town stoned him, another gave him the freedom of its streets. He fared no better and no worse than many Christian voyagers of the day. His one regret was that his shadow remained stubbornly unshrivelled, but he came to believe this had been allowed him as an aid for teaching. And sometimes it would speak to him on his solitary journeys.

Somewhere along the littoral arc that reaches up to the Greater Caucasus, he had arrived among a small tribe known as the Tlesi. By walking barefoot on their sacred mountain between dawn and dusk, he trampled the object of their worship. The following dawn they captured him and tied him to a tree. A close examination revealed the ChiRho tattooed minutely on his forehead. Though they had never seen this sign before, it confirmed their opinion that this was a foreign demon, come to threaten the power of their local god. According to their ritual practice, they cut off his penis with a sharpened stone and then gouged out his eyes with a spear. During all of this Aliochus did not call out to God, for he had preached too long that what is outside is inside, that if God is not within you then there is no God. Instead he asked his body to share with him the riddle of its pain.

When they had done with him they threw him from a near-by precipice. It had been a lean season and the resident fauna had his bones picked clean by sunset. By then the Tlesi had returned to their village and were starting on the feast prescribed after the successful slaughter of a demon.

The son of Aliochus sent the original of his gospel to the guide in Jerusalem, for he had given his father a solemn undertaking to do so. As far as is known, that text has never again be seen by human eyes. The copy Barbus made was not identical with the original. Though determined to carry out his father's will, the boy had much work of his own to do. He prided himself, though, on his remarkable memory. He therefore read his father's gospel carefully, despatched it as requested to the address in Jerusalem and, some months later, when he at last had some time to himself, he sat down to write out from memory the original text. He knew much of the story, of course, for he had studied hard at school. He had noticed some oddities in his father's version and found his mind shifting back to the pattern of his prime remembrance in the intervening months. Whenever he was in doubt as to how a particular part of the story went, he would go to see the scholar in the next town, who gave him access to his little library. Thus did the boy fill out the gaps.

Many centuries later this text was found by accident in a still readable condition. It was identified as a corrupt but essentially orthodox redaction, most likely from a Johannine community in Asia Minor. It is now one of the numbered codices in the Vatican Archive.

The Painter

Her fingers were like insects mating in the air. They came together in frenzies, then threw each other apart again. His eyes flicked between her face and her hands. They seemed to fill the whole room, leaving him there as no more than a spectator, on the outside, taking notes.

When she stopped talking, she turned back to her painting. The white circle which she had pressed straight from the tube on to the canvas was crooked, as though gravity were pressing it from all sides. And the surrounding aquamarine made it look like a calcium shell about to implode underwater. The vivid red was beginning to vein inside the egg as her fingers rushed at the shapes.

'I have never understood what they mean by abstract,' she said, her voice full of the lyric drawl of the southern states. 'A rose is abstract. What does it represent but itself? What's the mimesis of a leaf? An eye maybe, looking into the spectrum to see what makes it flourish, a green eye that the wind shakes water from. Why should I give you something on canvas you already have a roomful of at home? Why compete with God or Tiffany's? And who can afford the ground rent anyway?'

Her fingers shaped the space between her mouth and the picture. Each time she cupped her hand in that gesture her husband had once made so famous, he felt his own body rouse. Old photographs. Erotic memories from a time when he wasn't even born.

'Or maybe it's not me that you really want to talk about? Maybe you're being polite, like so many of them, waiting until you can finally ask about what you came to ask about. Mr Augustine Bentley.'

He said nothing and she began to attack the canvas with more rapid daubs. He started to see how she assembled the flashes of colour into the daytime of her easel before the rainbow disappeared.

'He was a better photographer than he was a man,' she said. 'And a much better photographer than he was a husband. Whereas I'd say I'm about as good at painting as I was at being a wife, or anything else for that matter. But the only photographs of me which anyone's ever interested in are the ones he shot before we married. So there's something for a man to ponder. Don't marry your model unless you want to start looking for another one straight away. That's what Augustine did. As soon as we were back from honeymooning in the Caribbean, he went and honeymooned some more in the Bronx. But this time he didn't take me with him. You've probably seen those pictures too, I'd imagine.'

He had. Everybody had. And she was right that it was impossible to look at her without seeing the photographs he had taken. She had to walk now through those black and white poses every time she entered a room. He had seen her in a certain way, a certain light, with no clothes to put her in parenthesis, and now every man who ever looked at her body measured her against those shots. Already age had contradicted the images she'd once provided. Already the white in her hair was silver backing showing through the mirror.

'One newspaper even asked if I'd take my clothes off again for them; sit in exactly the same pose as I did for Augustine, so they could do it again. I told them there was no again, not with the photographer, not with the photograph, and not with the model either. The reason people love those photographs is because of the love he put into them. Because he did love me then, you know. Or loved something he called by my name.'

She stopped painting for a moment and looked at the young man. Those great hazel eyes – he remembered the symmetrical whisper between the eyes and the nipples in two of Bentley's shots. She ran a hand down her smock and pulled it tight at the bottom. Her breasts were pendulous in the photographs, the slowest thing about her otherwise speeding and manic limbs. That was forty years ago. Who could know what she would look like now?

'As long as he wanted something there was a kind of magic he could find there, a crackle of static electricity in everything his eye touched. But the magic left the studio the minute we were married. Once he knew he had me, once I'd stopped pulling away from him in my mind and turned back towards him and told him I was his, the magic moved on to the streets. Then he did all those famous pictures of New York at dawn and twilight. And they're filled with love and longing too. A true eroticism, an eroticism of the street. Because by then, come dawn or twilight, where he wanted to be was out there on the streets. Always had to do the shots of what he loved. But then we all have to do that. Or what we do's not worth the trouble it takes to look at it.'

She stood back for a moment. Now inside the fractured white outline a frenzy of life had begun as she stitched the red and blue flecks into a mosaic battle between the warm and the cold, the fire and the ice.

'Now he's dead, it's strange,' she said. 'I see those photographs he took of me, and I'm looking at my own expression from so many years ago. I'm looking at myself, trying to find what it was in him that he was seeing. Because what he was seeing must have been me, or the me he wanted anyway. And I didn't know who that person was. I didn't know what it was that he desired. Nothing but the shadow of his own desire as it crossed my flesh. It was the shadow his camera made when he stood over me, mounted on the three legs of his tripod. Everybody knows that one. I even read somewhere how that shot introduces dialectics into photography. He'd have enjoyed that, I'm sure. As soon as I lit it all up with acceptance, and the shadows disappeared, he stopped desiring. There's more love in the photographs he did of yellow cabs than the ones he took of me after we were married. I made him destroy them. I'm not ready to pose dead yet, I told him. If you want pictures of corpses, go to the cemetery.'

One solitary thread of crimson had broken the white surround she had created. He could not work out if she had made a mistake. He couldn't ask her. He carried on making notes. She stared at that red breach in her white wall, looking puzzled.

'Always end up talking about him,' she said. 'People come here for an interview with me about my painting and we always end up talking about Augustine Bentley Esquire, sometime photographer of this planet. Can't escape him now. Thought finally when I put him into his grave I'd get away from it all at last. Went to a tiny South American fishing village and turned a little house there into a studio. It only took two months before *Time Magazine* turned up at the door. They were doing a retrospective article about the photography of Augustine Bentley and wanted me to help. I thought, you don't give up, do you Gus, even from the far side of the grave. You can't just let me get on with my painting. You have talent, he would say to me, you have talent but now you must work. It's strange how when people tell you that you have talent, what they're really saying is that you have no real achievement to match it.

'And you,' she said, turning round and facing him again, with the brush in her hand pointing upwards, 'would you rather look at my paintings, or the photographs of me without my clothes on which Augustine created all those years ago? Which one gives the supple body of your mind the most pleasure?'

'I like to look at both,' he said. He was a third her age.

'No woman should ever be photographed naked,' she said, turning back again to the canvas with even greater concentration. It seemed to him that she was letting the frenzy of the red overwhelm everything else in the picture. The red had started eating all the other colours now. 'Then she's given a mirror to time, so that time can look back at her all the way down her years. I would see it in their eyes, you know, the men I went with after Augustine. I'd see them look at me as the clothes came off, noting a sagging here and an ageing there, compared with those photographs, those silvery prints, those little frozen moments of old Augustine's dead desire. They couldn't help themselves. They wanted those photographs to come alive again. They never understood what a fiction they were in the first place. They're not a documentary record of a woman. They're the traces of Bentley's desperation, fixed by chemicals on to paper. Finally, I gave up altogether. I gave up trying to find out who it was that Bentley had seen when he first went hunting my flesh with those big lenses of his. And now, what does it matter anyway? At my age, what could it possibly matter?'

She was still as slim as she had been forty years ago, though, he could make out that much of the shape of her body beneath the paint-smeared smock.

'You will send me a copy of the article, won't you?' she said to him at the door.

'I will,' he said. He touched her hand. Those fingers, still electric with unstillness.

That night he turned the pages of the famous book, the book that had made Bentley's name as one of the great photographers of the century. She kept swerving out towards him with her troubled eyes, trying to see what the watcher had seen, that he should spend so much of his time watching her. And those extraordinary fingers clawing at the air as though it were flesh. In some she wore a small bowler hat and in others the white and black of silk and satin, which had given her once such a distinctive look, a nun whose frenzy would tear down the convent walls. Always clutching her clothes as though even the wind might unwrap them, clutching her throat as though sunlight might melt it. Then there on the next page she was once more unwrapped, wrapped and riddled only in her skin, eyes still asking their hungry questions in the silence of the book.

The next morning he started his article about her:

It is forty years since Augustine Bentley first photographed the naked body of his lover in a studio in Manhattan. He did not photograph her painting, but waiting: waiting to be photographed. Waiting until the eye of the lens had finished its business with her, so that she could at last put her clothes back on, and step into the world.

Doctor Freud and Mister Looney:
A Family Romance

The Doctor stood at the window and watched the man get out of the cab. An old man. Another old man. It was a mistake for one old man to meet another, for he would see nothing in his guest's features but a mirror, the grey mirror the grave holds up as you walk towards it. Strachey and Jones had both told him that he was not to be seen publicly associating with this Mr Looney, whom the English thought intellectually disreputable. So he had arranged for the fellow to come to his home quietly in the evening, so as to create no fuss. Now his jaw was once more causing him excruciating pain and he wished he could be left to himself. Duty and courtesy would, as always, prevail.

Anna showed him in.

'Mr Looney.'

'Dr Freud.'

'Please sit down. You would like some tea? Anna, perhaps . . .' The faithful daughter was already on her way to make it. Few men had ever been blessed with such a daughter. Freud looked hard at the schoolteacher from

Gateshead and realised that he was disappointed. He examined this emotion briefly and realised it came from a coalescence of subject and author in his expectations. Which was to say that the man who had written *Shakespeare Identified* and thereby established that the author of the works of 'Shakespeare' was not the nondescript of Stratford but the 17th Earl of Oxford, should not himself have looked quite so . . . nondescript.

'First, Dr Freud, let me express my deepest commiseration for your plight in having to flee your Vienna.'

'Not my Vienna,' Freud said, as the prosthesis cut sharply into his mouth. 'It was never that, I can assure you. The city is a beautiful lady who would never have married a Jew. Now she is making use of Karl Luger's dowry to marry a German. He has very loud boots.'

Looney felt a little lost by this, but he knew that his companion had recently suffered much. The newspaper reports said that some members of his family were still over there, unable to escape. And the news grew worse by the day. He felt he had to greet his eminent companion more warmly. He took from his briefcase his book and handed it to the Doctor.

'Please receive this inscribed copy of my work, as a token of the esteem in which I hold you.'

Freud opened the book at the title page. Looney had written: *To Dr Freud. Perhaps the most eminent of all my admirers.*

'Perhaps,' Freud said quietly. 'Vielleicht.'

Anna brought the tea and poured it for them. She

explained to Mr Looney that her father could not spend longer than thirty minutes in conversation. That was an unbreakable rule of his physician's. He might require another operation the following week. Freud was grateful for her remarks. She had seen that look of weariness in his face, even though he tried to hide it.

'Of course, of course,' Looney said. 'I myself have a train to catch back to Gateshead. I have been visiting the British Museum.'

Anna left the room in silence. Freud stared at the man's face. There was something indistinct about it. It lacked a focus. Not like the young fellow, what was his name, Salvador Dali, who had visited him last week. He had never seen such a consummate example of the Spaniard before. The man was a complete fanatic.

'It has always intrigued me, Dr Freud, why you were first drawn to my work.'

Freud was back momentarily in Berggasse, back in those days he'd spent consolidating the great discoveries.

'I had seen a classic Oedipus complex at work in the figure of Hamlet,' he said. 'It was an extreme example of ambivalence: the prince is obligated to kill his mother's husband, the man who has killed his own father so that he can occupy the queen's bed. But something stops him, constantly stops him. This Renaissance prince, who is capable of anything, cannot carry out the commands of his own murdered father. Why not? Because of his identification with Claudius in terms of what Claudius has enacted.

Claudius, you see, has done precisely what Hamlet himself wished to do: murder his father so that he can enjoy his mother sexually. To kill Claudius would be effectively to kill himself. It is interesting how early in the play he reflects upon suicide – always a sign that there are data in excess of what the conscious ego is able to manipulate. When Hamlet does finally kill Claudius, of course, he dies almost simultaneously. And by the same means. Poison is the most insidious of the lethal weapons. It constitutes an invisible aggression.'

Mr Looney had put down his teacup.

'That is entirely fascinating,' he said. 'But forgive me, I don't see necessarily where my discoveries . . .'

'I had no doubt', Freud continued, 'that the Hamlet figure had been created subsequent to the death of the author's own father. There is such a cathexis in the figure of the ghost. Prior to 1921 I had no reason to doubt that Shakespeare's father had died prior to the composition of the play. However, at that time a new edition of Brandes's *William Shakespeare* appeared. A note had been discovered which established that *Hamlet* had been performed prior to 1601, when Shakespeare's father died. This left my interpretation of the play in a problematical condition. Then I came across your book.

'It was convincingly argued, of course, and were Edward de Vere to be the author of the work we call "Shakespeare" then the fact that his father died while he was a child and that his mother contracted another marriage which led the young de Vere to repudiate her – well, all of this consolidates my thesis. Then there were other things too. The Earl of Oxford sired three daughters, but was too improvident to be able to provide for them. This would explain the strange ambivalence of Lear's giving away his kingdom to three daughters, who subsequently repudiate him.'

'Two, I think,' Looney said, smiling. Freud stared at him.

'He gave away his kingdom to two daughters who repudiated him. He tried to give it away to three, though, you're quite right.'

Freud took a sip of the tea. Looney felt he had offended him by interrupting. It struck the schoolmaster what a noble physiognomy the psychoanalyst had. The grey beard and penetrating eyes had now combined with the clenched and suffering jaw. Freud's stoicism in regard to his own pain had combined with his melancholy examination of the viciousness of mankind to produce at the end a strange radiance about his features.

'So, in a sense,' Looney ventured, 'the data as presented were contradicted by your own scientific discoveries.'

'Precisely,' Freud said, feeling very weary now and hoping the visit would not be unnecessarily extended. Looney was warming to his theme.

'I myself came to the conclusion that the low-bred impostor from Stratford was no more than that, after applying the scientific precepts of Auguste Comte. An examination of the work in the light of these made it evident that, among other things, the man simply had to be a member of the higher aristocracy. This was quite evident from the internal evidence of the plays: the mastery of courtly life, the knowledge of Italy, the grasp of the niceties of falconry. I then went from "Venus and Adonis" to Palgrave's *Golden Treasury* and found "Women", the poem by de Vere. Same stanzaic forms, same repeated rhythms. That set me on the trail of de Vere and everything I subsequently discovered confirmed my first impressions.

'Technically, of course, I had no expertise in these matters at all. It needed someone from outside the field to see what others who were too close to the material could not.'

Freud looked at the man with a renewed interest.

'There are a few problems, Jones tells me,' the Doctor said.

'Oh, that business about *The Tempest*. I wouldn't say problems. Internal evidence certainly shows that *The Tempest* was written after de Vere's death. The play does not, however, belong in the canon. The verse is tawdry and doesn't scan, and the philosophy it expresses amounts to second-hand materialism. It is so hard, though, to get people to take off their blinkers. But I need not tell that to you, Dr Freud.'

'No indeed.'

'Much is hidden to protect the cant of the common man. You know that when I first submitted my book to the publisher it was accepted only on condition that I publish it under a *nom de plume*.'

'And why was that?'

'Because the groundlings might scoff at a book authored
by a man named Looney.'

'A diminutive of lunatic in the vulgar tongue?'

'Precisely. I do, in fact, have noble ancestors myself,'
Looney continued with another smile. 'My family is
descended from the Earl of Derby. They were once kings of
the Isle of Man.'

Freud could disguise his weariness no longer. He could
also hear Anna coughing outside the door.

'I myself have no noble forebears,' he said. 'Though
perhaps I have given birth to a noble line.'

Looney looked at him with evident incomprehension.

'The science of psychoanalysis,' he said. 'One of its
discoveries, incidentally, was the family romance. Are you
aware of that particular psychological manoeuvre?'

Looney shook his head. 'No. I'm sorry I haven't managed
to read as much of your work as . . .'

'The child, unhappy with its parents and its position, posits
a hidden family from which it has been separated. This family
is of noble birth. Thus, in the repudiation of its own
humdrum parentage, the child asserts its more elevated
lineage and provides as well the reason for the incomprehension of its needs.'

'Is such a family romance inevitable?'

'It is certainly very common.'

'Then sooner or later the children of your own new line
will repudiate their father and claim that such a noble science

could not possibly have been created by . . .' Here Looney faltered.

'By a bourgeois Jew from Vienna,' Freud said. 'Believe me, the process has already started. A young man I once trusted and who told me on a boat sailing to America that I was *kein Menschenkenner* is proving that he was correct, in that one regard, if no other.'

Here Anna came in carrying Mr Looney's coat. The schoolmaster stood up.

'I really must be leaving, Dr Freud. It has been the greatest possible pleasure.'

The two men shook hands. Freud bowed gently. Then he turned round and went over to his bookshelf. He took down one of the volumes there and wrote something in it. He handed the book to Looney.

'Please take this as a token of my own esteem.'

That night Dr Freud wondered once more about the wisdom of publishing, at this hour of peril for his people, his discovery that Moses was not a Jew at all, but a high-born Egyptian. Mr Looney sat in the train carriage staring through the window for a long time before he took the book which Freud had given him out of his bag. It was the first edition of *The Interpretation of Dreams*. On the title page Freud had written 'From Sigm. Freud. Your most eminent admirer. Vielleicht.' Mister Looney felt his cheeks warm. He turned the pages. The book was unfortunately printed in

German, a language his own forays into the realms of scholarship had never yet obliged him to acquire.

Intelligent Terminal

Kline was distracted. What distracted him was the worst source of irritation after illness: money. The cause of the second worst distraction was in fact the first, though the illness belonged thankfully not to him but to his father. His father was not ill. No, that word, ashen and hospital sheeted as it was, still plinked into a bucket of hope, mild and optimistic. Kline's father was dying. Having drunk his way through life, he was now drinking his way into death with the same systematic appetite. As far as Kline could see, his father was as blithe regarding his present condition as he had been in respect of all the previous ones. He lay in his bedroom reading (for he was a great reader) and drinking. Kline's mother decanted the liquor into various medical-type containers. Even she had now accepted the forthcoming death. Well, the death of the body, anyway. The source of Kline's distraction was his mother's commitment to the preservation of his father's mind, and that meant money, and not just a plink in a bucket either. It meant all the money the family had.

Kline finished edging his tie under his mauve collar. He

flicked a fingernail of cream on to his hair. At thirty he was presentable, fit, not beautiful, but he didn't like beautiful men, or women either for that matter. He might want them sometimes, but he didn't like them, the way they entered each room as though arriving to complete it, the one decoration required for all else to fall into place.

The template in his driver's window acknowledged recognition and he was inside speaking quietly to the console, which remarked his stress quotient. He said he knew and required no further bio-comments. The car took him through the sector (which he hated) and he looked out over the ruined canals and bombed-out railway sidings, over the old metal cars slowly oxidising. Capitalist production. And, of course, the dead computers, old screens like square-eyed cyclopses blind without their electricity, scattered over the margins of the road. Nothing more dead than last year's intelligence unit.

His sister lived here, he supposed as some sort of protest, to escape the code. She said it was just the money, but he didn't believe her. The social monitor didn't obtain here, so she could have her one-nighters with Flecks who were fleeing one sector after another for salvage, without being mandated for scans and screenings. It made him angry, all of it. And now that he was actually here again, it made him slightly sick.

The air was thick in this part of town. The Prefects claimed there weren't sufficient resources to windmill all the sectors, but no one believed this. If you're dissident, you eat offal and breathe faecal stench, seemed to be the official policy, one that he was more than happy to go along with, as a matter of fact. But because of his sister he had actually to come here. Not often, it was true, but a zero-count would have suited him better. There'd be one more trip after this for the funeral. Then she could do what she liked, jive her Flecks in the middle of Route Thirteen for all he cared.

He pressed the parcel charge on his console. Not receiving. That's all he needed. The block she was in was gothed most nights, and the copper from the antique circuitry was always the first thing to go. He engaged security and got out. It was like dropping into a sewer. The smell slapped him. He hurried through the atrium (unlit, of course) and ran up the two flights to her door. From previous trips he knew it was pointless to press for the lift. Even if it were working, there'd be people in there you didn't want to meet.

She was only half-dressed. The possibility flashed before him that she might have a Fleck in there, that some great shambling bearded apparition might ghost through the door to show him the purple tattoo and grin. She saw him looking to the bedroom.

'It's all right, brother. There's no one here but me.'

'Managed to do without it for one night, did you?'

She lifted her shift to tutu position and fluttered over to him, ballet style. She leaned her chin on his shoulders and whispered, 'I suppose you manage to do without it all the time now, do you, brother? Or maybe you find the scans and

surveillances and electronic ID in the hospital's Eros department has started to turn you on?'

'Get dressed, sister, and let's get out of this slurry hole
before someone goths my Cruiser.'

She dressed deliberately like one of the old-style tarts, the
ones in the electronic library. He couldn't imagine where she
found the material. The stockings, the red skirt, the
bandanna, the crimson lipstick, the coal-black shadow. He
kept turning to look at her as the Cruiser accelerated.

'Interested, brother? You should come over one Friday.
I'm not the only girl round here with access to period desire.
Or was it the incest that added extra piquancy?'

'The Eros Archives. It's illegal, you know.'

She laughed. 'We operate on the basis that everything we
do is illegal. We'd be surprised if anything wasn't. So what
will you do if they stop us to look me over?'

'I'll say it's a film', he said, 'for the centre. I'm working on
one. I have the ID.'

He turned and stared at her again. He could see the point,
perhaps for the first time. He caught that scent of danger and
arousal, but it couldn't (surely?) be worth the risk.

'Shouldn't you be watching where we're going?'

'The Cruiser's self-control,' he said, turning back.

'Money, my brother. Where did that come from, I
wonder?'

'It hasn't come from anywhere yet,' he said.

They glided up through Route Thirteen with the Cruiser
fluently avoiding the debris, mechanical, electronic and
human, that raddled this old road through the ancient
wharves. In the distance towers flashed through the fog.
Other Cruisers took off and landed.

'You know what all this is about?' he said.

'Mummy wants to re-create daddy.'

'Not the deposit option though. Entire activation.'

'Money money money,' she said merrily. 'Is there
enough?'

'Just. There's always just enough after the activation boys
have done their sums. A triple mortgage here, an option on
posthumous credits there. It will clear out the family fund.'

'So no money for my little brother Kline to pay off his
self-control Cruiser, or pay for a deregulated wife.'

'No money for you either,' he said, angrily. She was
enjoying herself now.

'I never expected any, brother dear. I get by.'

'Your Flecks pay, I suppose?'

'They pay. We all pay. But my requirements are modest.
They used to say that time was money. Now there's no time,
is there, brother, so what do you need money for, anyway?'

She was laughing. He looked at her teeth. How did she
manage to keep them so white, living where she did and
how she did? God, he hated her.

He was in the De-Periodisation Unit of Cinematics. It was
true, though a crude way of putting it, that there was no
longer any time in the old sense. That had been based on a

now-defunct momentum, which had once led to a series of misunderstandings, now being comprehensively wiped. Biblical linearities, Enlightenment progressives, Darwin aetiologies – all in different ways missing entirely the fact of simultaneity, thereby resulting in a near-total occlusion of knowledge.

He had done some work on the iconography of the observers, eyes pressed to telescopes to stare at the pulsating discs of light; eyes pressed to microscopes to stare at the pulsating squirms of viruses. Odd how they had never understood their median position. Or how it required that the emptiness of the universe had to be filled up with time.

But now time was a false context, throwing up censored notions like solution, conflict, history. At the Unit they were presenting the facts, cut free from the illusions of temporality. At present he was regrading the atrocities. Freed from time-cant and consequently dated binaries like life/death, pain/comfort, win/lose, they had become simply another statistical resource.

They were nearing Seven, where their parents lived. A moment's flash of light (he thought it might be sun, but it seemed unlikely) lit up the needles in the gravel. The Cruiser berthed, landed them and took itself off to one of the stages.

'Kline you look so . . . new,' his mother said and kissed him, then she turned to his sister.

'And you look so . . .'

'Don't say old, mother, it's disallowed.'

'She's doing an educational, mother,' Kline said. He wanted all this over with. Conflict itself was no more than a species of time-entrapment. It could be avoided. They went through to the bedroom. Monitors. Basins. Towels. Syringes. And the big blue bottles that she poured the sharp gold liquid into. His father's body was thinned by the ravaging. His eyes were closed. His features had grown oddly luminous with an exactness of purpose. Death had been tuning him up for its own silent ends.

'They're here, Father,' she said.

Slowly the eyes opened and the grave-sheet blank of his face unfolded into a stoical smile. He looked for a long time at Kline's sister, up and down.

'Soho,' he said. 'Nineteen seventy.'

'No dates, Dad,' Kline said.

'Pass me my bootleg anaesthetic, will you?'

He was propped up and given a large coloured beaker.

'Your mother thinks that if she puts my Scotch in these rainbow containers, everyone will think I'm sipping alkaline solutions. But everyone knows what it is I've been drinking these last forty years, even that evil little nurse with the tape recorder in her tights. I think it might be the only thing she does have in there.'

'Father!' Mother hated him talking that way. He started laughing, but the laugh turned into a cough. Mother held him. He took another jag at the whisky.

'Right,' he said finally, 'let's get on with it.'

Mother smoothed herself down and started.

'Well, as you know, with daddy's illness, we have to be practical and think of the future.'

'There isn't any,' the old man said, 'it's all been a misunderstanding. Kline can explain that to you.'

'Think of the present, Mother,' Kline said.

'We must think of the present, that's right. So we've decided . . .'

'You've decided,' Kline's father said.

'*We've* decided. Decided that we don't want to lose him. Or rather that the category of losing him has now become defunct, as the young man explained to us.'

'They want to computerise me,' Kline's father said, 'so that when I die, I don't.'

'That's another category the young man said is defunct,' Kline's mother said, growing more cheerful with each sentence now. 'Daddy can be with us as much as he is now. His face. His voice. His humour.'

'Have they taught the console how to drink moonshine yet, Mother?' Kline's sister asked. Her father started laughing again.

'That's not a nice thing to say. Not nice at all,' her mother said. But Kline's sister and father were both chuckling now. Kline was impatient.

'How much?' he said.

'That's my boy,' his father said. 'No flies on my son Kline, eh? However many there might be on me soon.'

'Flies don't eat hardware, Father,' Kline's sister said, still laughing. 'It's non-biodegradable. They'd break their little teeth.'

'Everything,' Kline's father said, suddenly unsmiling and looking straight at him. 'It will cost everything.'

'What's the point?' Kline said.

'What's the point?' his mother echoed. 'What's the point? So that I won't be left alone here, that's what's the point. So that I'll still have someone. And you can still have your father.'

'Do it,' Kline's sister said. 'We don't want the money do we, brother? We'd rather mummsy was happy wouldn't we, brother? Then we can snoodle over and hash over old times with pops here, can't we, Kline?'

'There are no old times,' Kline said wearily, knowing now he was defeated. 'If it is recollected, it is collected; what can be remembered is already a member. If you're remembering the past, then you are simply addressing the present by an illusory name.'

'That's what the young man said,' Kline's mother said brightly. 'That's exactly what he said. So daddy doesn't die.'

'I simply move from here to there,' said Kline's father, pointing to the console with the hand that wasn't holding the drink. 'I don't even need to get resurrected, because I don't die. I merely slide from this decrepit system to that entirely functioning one. Look at it gleam. Much neater than that business with Jesus. And you won't even have to wait three days for me to shout Peek-a-Boo.'

Kline turned to look at his sister, whose eyes did not shift from her father's face.

'Daddy,' she said softly, 'the only one of you I didn't lose.'

2

The self-control Cruiser went back to the suppliers and Kline was once more driving manual guides. His anger modulated into a more containable disgust. He worked on the Atrocity Project. The episode was called Weapons to Flesh. Since the psychology unit had finished its organum on conscience-wipes, individual actions were no longer factored in the statistics. The calculus of gun/blade/chemical distribution to flesh entry-points or nervous systems now made an interesting and intelligible graph. Again with the babble of history discounted, together with any false consciousness of temporality, everything was present to the understanding. It was Kline's job to devise visual means of conveying this. There would, after all, be no money coming from any other source.

In his archive lay the cartography of torment and slaughter, a cliometric of the tortured cries of children, the vastly detailed topography of annihilation. None of this was fully possible to assimilate until the emotions generated through time disappeared along with time itself. The archive film material showed grown men who wept to remember the numbers, the mountain of uncountable numbers. Now all the data was finally amassed and computed, it was awesome (like accounts of geological formations) but foreign to them all, beyond the credibilities of their delimited emotions, and certainly beyond the statutory emotions specified for the time segments. Kline was still startled, though, by these concentrations of misery scattered over the earth's skin. These Dachau memories, these Auschwitz memories, these Belsen ghost memories, these Katyns and Kampucheas and Rwandas would still blink in pixels of astonishment, even from his bland screen, even in the ahistoric rainbow of those processed colours.

Drained entirely of time, these stains of association would one day rinse away entirely. But Kline could still read time in them. Time, the last great age of civilisation. What was still unanswerable was how they could have so misread the signs. All the clues had been provided, starting with their culture's first breath. Aristotle had written: Time cannot exist without a soul to count it. Still they did not see that when time became an automatism weighted with the squat machines of murder and modernity, it rolled away from that soul like a toy from a careless child, stalled, then started to roll back. All the stunned chronologies gazing out from clockfaces, calendars, and digital machines alerted hardly anyone. By that stage man had grown so deaf inside the helmet of his artifice, he could not even hear how the ticks thumping away in his own chest were all pointing backwards.

The gravest mistake was the notion they had developed that, because of the aetiology of their technologies, time itself could only ever move forwards. For a whole century the faces of their own atrocities had stared out to tell them how time, inside their own sectors, was already turning back. Of course they mistook the progress of omega collations – like the growing decrepitude of biologicals – for irreversible time-indicators. They are, as we now know, entirely different.

Some theorists linked the stalling and reversal of time directly to the atrocities. The holes ripped in the earth to tip men, women and children into ever since the Great War had torn gaps in the continuum. Armenia, the Shoah, the Gulag, Hiroshima, Cambodia, Rwanda: all those victims who were either marched out of time, or given only time to eat. And the strange conversion of their ideologies of hope to cruelty, so that even Marxism joined in the expulsion from time of those deemed to have erroneously intruded into it, those accused of occupying the wealth of space. Other theorists insisted that the iconographic inertia of photography impinged on time's momentum; that the ceaseless halting and tripping of time through lenses fatally slowed it.

Certainly the homogeneous spread of time so blithely promoted now seems incredible. Though alerted by the Einsteinian space–time continuum, they continued to regard their own historic and emotional time as entirely sequential and linear, misled even here by what was in front of their faces, for sexuality with its insistent peripeteia structured through entanglement to climax led them falsely into narratology, when what they really required was a poetics of catastrophe.

Kline was intrigued in his loop trawls to discover how often the poets and artists had understood. Mandelstam knew early how time had stalled: he spoke of his age as a beast with its back broken, staring backwards at its own tracks.

The film-maker Tarkovsky (no accident that he was another Russian) had even entitled his book on cinema, *Sculpting in Time*, yet the point was not taken: how can you sculpt something that is moving? (The film theorist Ennius once claimed that film, exposed to time, even stationary time, could never again be fully wiped of it. When he went on to speculate in something like the same manner about the human mind, he was swiftly removed.)

Tarkovsky himself grew obsessed with the moment in the Book of Revelation when the Seventh Seal is opened and there is silence in heaven. And what happens? Nothing. This was the nothing the children of modernity preoccupied themselves with so neurotically for two centuries. All written out for them by the poet of Patmos.

Whatever the specific determinants or overdeterminants, the homologous structure was ruptured between time and that womb inside the vacancy once known (without any irony then) as humanity. With every iron and electronic hare they set running faster and faster, they split time's motivation, until, divided into two hemispheres, time stalled. Then rolled back one inch. The rest (the one story that isn't archived, since no one can bring themselves to touch that boulder of radioactive time) is known. To you as well as to us. Even though we have agreed to forget it in advance.

Kline was cataloguing the Cassandra Voicings, that long, insistent wail from the sanity/insanity binary which led invariably to incarceration. Again, Kline was trawling the literary remnants. It intrigued him how clear the messages were in the classical texts. Freud realised this and then (characteristically) chose the wrong myths. The voicings came screaming off the page in Shakespeare, with Hamlet and Edgar having to adopt madness as a strategy for survival, and Lear only finding reality at all after he lost his wits. But there was the terrible noise of time that Mandelstam heard. The bigger and louder the scope of their noise, with generators hurling their sounds into the darkness of space, so great dishes could throw them back again, the more entropic and dwarfed their language became. Technical wizardry, linguistic midgetry. In the vertiginous babble of the Cassandra Voicings, the protest could have been heard at any time. But nobody listened.

Kline saw the screen grow bright again with the sites of the institutions, and the statistics of the silencings, the needles and the drugs. A whole continent of the insane, choking inside their own skins. Again he was impressed how many of the writers and artists were with them, choosing a kaleidoscope of annihilations before untruth. He whistled quietly.

Celia Greenock was at his shoulder.

'Everything all right?'

'Yes,' he said, 'an inadvertent hiss.'

'Sounded like an exclamation.' Celia stared at him. She was small, thin, with close-cropped blonde hair. She had once invited him to couple, but the prospect of the clinic and the monitors had dissuaded him. She had no emotions about this, of course, since none were permitted, though it seemed to Kline that she had pursued her invigilatory duties subsequently with an exemplary zeal.

'What would I exclaim at?' Kline said evenly.

'Zando started exclaiming at the archive when he had this job.'

'Yes, and now he's in the Snow Sector.'

'That's precisely why I was concerned,' Celia said. 'It's hardly as though the screen is a deregulated wife, is it?'

'Unfortunately not,' Kline said, with a philosophic smile. Money.

3

It was worth one last try. His father could well be so bored with the process, he might be persuaded to cancel. The insurance at this stage would still be valid. He drove over to Seven. His mother opened the door.

'Oh hallo, darling. Come in. They're about to finish for the day.' His mother looked younger already. The eternal option of the programme had evidently rejuvenated her.

The young analyst came through the bedroom door.

'Mr Gyron, this is my son Kline,' his mother said.

'Hi.'

'How are you getting on with the old man?'

'Fine. He's an exemplary case. All surface memory, no repression. We project some indicators through the day, and at night the dream monitor collects all the information we need. Two more weeks and we should be done.'

'He'll last that long will he?' Kline asked.

'I would have thought. Still seems quite strong. If not, I have enough data for emergency collation. He'd be near-perfect. A few mangled responses, perhaps.'

'That would probably be even more realistic,' Kline said.

'Kline, really. Like his father, his sense of humour is a little . . .'

'Diseased,' the analyst said without smiling. 'Your husband's won't be anyway, not after the transposition.'

Kline sat at the side of the bed. His father drank from a luminous pink tumbler.

'If you've come to talk me out of it, I'm afraid you're too late.'

'The concept "too late" is now inoperative, Father.'

'And the concept "now" is now too late. It was your mother's idea not mine. But now I've started, I'll finish it. Now I've put all this work in, I'm curious to find out who I'll be. Maybe I'll feel a little better.'

'You understand what they do?' Kline said, using now the only weapon he had left — his knowledge.

'What do they do, Kline? For once in your life tell me something I don't know.'

'It's part of the project, but they don't want to have to pay for it all. So they encourage as many people as possible to subscribe to the transposition, then you pay for it and they get the benefit.'

'How will they get the benefit?'

'You're keyed through to Central Intelligence and Statistics. All your data will be monitored.'

'But what do they want to know about me?' his father asked.

'Same as they want to know about everyone else: reactions to the abolition of time. The way they once studied what happened to the spacemen when they took gravity away. No one knows how long it persists. They've started to worry now, that when they split all those atoms, time was already leaking then. We've never known, you see, what contained time. Maybe nothing. Maybe time contained us. In which case we're being unwrapped. They want to know if, even outside an omega collation like the body, time can persist in traces.

'So once fully transposed, you'll be rid of the vertigo factor of tenses. Technically you'll be cleansed of all preterite infections. There'll be no more discrete momentums left. You will be approved synchronicity. But they'll be listening in, just to make sure you are.'

His father was offering him a blue beaker. He hesitated.

'Go on, for God's sake, Kline. It's probably the last time you'll ever see me.'

Kline took the glass and drank some of the whisky. It

scorched the inside of him. There was some memory, some trace . . .

'So I'll be plugged in to Central Intelligence, will I? Non-stop? Then that'll be my first chance to tell them what I think, and this time they'll have to listen.'

'But you don't understand, Dad . . .'

'I've promised your mother I'd meet her again in the future.'

'The present,' Kline said, standing up to leave.

'What?'

'It's the present you're going to meet her in. All the other places have been closed down.'

4

The programming back in Seven continued, so he was told. He couldn't be bothered going to find out. If he hadn't already discarded his with/without dichotomy, he might have thought that he would very happily do without the presence of his father, for the sake doing something with the money. But, as another meaningless locution had it, too late now. (If it's now, it goes without saying, it can't be too late.)

One night he received a message from his sister. Why didn't he come over to meet some of her friends? It was Friday.

It was true what his sister had said about the deregulated wife. Without money, it was hopeless. Without money, the regulation exceeded the desire, it was as simple as that. So people used electronic peripherals, and because they were Centre-controlled and Centre-directed the ones on release at any one time were limited. The people he worked with would often turn out to have been using the same one the night before. Though it was a sign he'd not gone completely clear, this somehow nauseated him. He concentrated on his Atrocity Project, but he was no monk. Now here he was driving through the sector on a Friday night. The fact that he was reduced to driving a manual Cruiser made him feel slightly easier. You'd have to be desperate to want to goth one of those.

He picked her up. She was in black, all black. The widow of desire. A veil like a spider's web across her face, and black crepe gloves all the way up to her elbows.

'Where?' he said.

'14.21.000.'

'Legal?'

'Nothing here's legal, brother. If it's legal you want, get out of the sector.' She crossed her legs and he could see where the black stocking ended and her white thigh started. Would he have to watch her getting picked up by a Fleck? What, he wondered, was he doing here? They arrived at the place. It must once have been a warehouse of some kind. He couldn't believe the authorities would come anywhere near this, but the position of his vehicle on central tracking could make them ask questions. He had brought the scroll camera with him. A few loops would cover him. He had been researching a project. His sister was temporary research assistant. They might buy it.

Inside was noise and colour of a sort you could only find in the sector now. They said it once leaked right across the town. Once. He caught himself saying it. Time entrapment. Ghost concepts bending his mind. The only drink was coloured gin. He bought two. They were strong. She was looking at him through the smoked light.

'My friends will be here soon. Get us another drink,' his sister said.

When the two friends came, he bought them drinks too, then sat at the table and stared at them. It was hard for him to focus on it, but he started to see that as they wiped time outside the sector, it must in some way be intensifying here. He had studied them in archive film he had filleted and destroyed. It wasn't just the clothes. He could swear that their faces too . . . Their voices were the old voices, they still had that singing laughter wrapped inside them. His sister was looking at him and smiling.

'You can feel it, can't you, brother? Now maybe you understand that when you say, How can I live here? I could only truthfully answer, How can you live there?'

The Flecks started arriving. Each one showed the purple mark on his arm to the doorlens. They stood in a huddle at the edge of the bar. Kline's sister's friends went over to them, but she stayed there looking at him.

'You could always join us, brother,' she said. 'You could

be our protector. A girl needs a protector. You could protect the three of us. The other girls would be very grateful. They'd take you for walks down Memory Lane. There's a little shelter at the bottom of it. Very dark. At night-time you can hear little cries come from it. Little sighs and cries as though a small furry animal were dreaming and calling out in its sleep. Think about it, brother. Demolition man. Are you sure you want to fix your head so firmly one way that it can't turn round on your shoulders?'

She was suddenly gone. He was half-dreamed with the gin and the words and the noise. She was over with her friends and the crowd of Flecks. Without thinking about it, he lifted the scroll camera into position behind the slit in his lapel and filmed them all as they shifted to the dance-pit and started.

They were snakes. Luminous. Writhing. He saw the patterns of their colours shift up and down against the forest. A part of him was not wiped. He would have thought this could have shown up on a monitor back at Centre, but for now he didn't care. What he could see you couldn't get on any electronic peripheral. A hand on his shoulder. He turned round. It was a Fleck. He flinched away, the loathing was programmed.

'Your Cruiser? Outside?' He nodded. 'Goths.'

Kline dropped whatever had been going in his head and ran for the door, but by the time he was outside they had already stripped it. He phoned through automatically without even thinking. He told the officer the co-ordinates.

There was a silence. Kline had started according to procedure with his authorisation code. Now the brigade had to come. It was regulations. Kline couldn't afford to fail insurance, or he would be grounded. But as he switched the phone off he realised what he'd done. He hurried back into the club and found his sister. She looked at him and bit her lip.

'Why did I have to bring you down here, brother? Just one night and you have to get the slime involved. You'd better clear out. There might be some angry people around soon.'

By the time the brigade arrived, the lights had gone out at the club. The music had stopped. There was no one to be seen.

The two uniformed men climbed out of the micro-light. They looked about them uneasily, then came over to Kline.

'This the reported Cruiser then?'

'Yes,' Kline said, trying to smile. 'Pretty mess, isn't it?'

The men took pictures and notes. Finally one asked the question Kline knew was coming.

'What exactly are you doing here, sir, at this time of night?'

'Research,' Kline said automatically.

The officers looked at each other, then back at Kline.

'Elaborate, if you would. Define, if possible,' the taller man said. Kline was afraid. The brigade had always frightened him, but then he didn't know anyone who wasn't frightened of them. He quickly explained his position, his work on the Atrocity Project, that he was on a reconnaissance for what might be a new project.

'Which project?' the smaller man said.

'The Eros Archive,' he said.

'Special passes required for any work there,' the tall man said, 'have one, do you?'

'I'm sorry, I've got behind on my paper work,' Kline said. He was getting desperate now. He reached behind his lapel and detached the scroll camera.

'Look,' he said, 'it's a Centre camera. They're only available on official lease.'

The smaller man looked at the camera intently.

'Yes,' he said, 'yes, this is official issue. Cinematographic ordnance. Unless you've stolen it, of course.'

'If I'd stolen it,' Kline said, 'do you imagine I would show it to you, after phoning you in?'

'That's true, I suppose,' the taller man said. 'Well, we'll take the camera and have you checked out, sir. If everything's in order, it will be returned to you tomorrow. Evidence of your research on there, is it?'

'Yes,' Kline said.

Later he called her. She screamed at him.

'You've got to get out,' he said.

'I've got nowhere to go, you fool. If they put a sector alert out for me, they'll find me wherever I am. They can route every Fleck I've been with for the last year, if they start scanning. We only survive here because no one pays any attention to us.'

'Come here,' he said. 'I'll hide you here.'

'I'd rather die in this part,' she said. 'Someone unwiped walking among you people – they can smell us.' She hung up. He called again later. There was no answer.

The brigade interviewed him twice. Then they gave him back the camera. An inspector took him for a little walk away from the other officers.

'You have been reckless, sir, very reckless indeed. It could have cost you your job and worse. But we understand.'

Kline looked into the man's face. A worn professional face, ragged round the eyes. A lifetime's service. The inspector smiled.

'One of your colleagues at the Centre gave us the information we needed, sir. You had spoken to him about the girl, your sister, living where she did, consorting with Flecks, consistent monitor-evasion and all the rest. It was brave of you to try, sir, but our data suggests she's now an incorrigible. On the run in any case. Try to put it to one side. The scroll film was your precaution presumably, in case you were attacked? Sensible. At least we might have found your killers. We'll keep it now. Part of the archive.'

Kline's sister wasn't at the body translation. Kline told his mother she'd been mandated into a far sector for some important work and couldn't be contacted. Secrecy obtained. His mother smiled, but she had never been difficult to lie to:

she always wanted to think the best of her family. Afterwards they sat in the living room.

'Any of dad's medicine left?' he asked.

'Oh well . . .'

'He'd have wanted us to,' he said.

'No,' she said, her face luminous with faith, 'he *wants* us to. Don't ever use the past tense again in this home about your father. He activated as the dust was slotted.'

They sat and drank the whisky. Posthumous whisky, Kline thought. Since his sister disappeared, all his modes were erroneous.

'Do you want to go and talk to him?' his mother said. 'It's just that I feel a little shy. Silly really. But it's like I felt on my wedding night. It's as though everything is new all over again, and I don't know quite what to expect.'

Kline walked through to the bedroom with his drink. On the console screen his father's features glowed, all health restored to them now, healthier than he had ever seen him in the bodily state. His head moved gently round with an unaccustomed grace and a Buddha's seraphic smile lit his features.

'Kline.'

Kline looked at the screen uneasily. There was something compelling about the eyes and the way they scanned him.

'Father.'

'Would you like me to help you back into the present?'

This was his father's voice and yet it seemed to him there was something about the benevolence that was inexplicably menacing. The softness of the words seemed to surround him.

'I'm in the present, Father. Where else could I be?'

Again the eyes seemed to penetrate deeper than his father's had ever done before. In life, his father had never looked at him for longer than a few seconds before turning away.

'Don't say in life,' his father said from the screen. But Kline had not said anything. In the small of his back he felt his sister's sharpened nail press in. 'Don't say in life. This is life, Kline. It's not elsewhere. There is no other. Old myths of time, old myths of Eros. There is no memory lane, Kline, the road has been demolished. Now it's one of the new routes and the most beautiful of them all. Their eyes don't mean it, my son: paradise is artificial, not that old reek of time. Why walk among diseases? You're half-scanned into coming clear. Don't turn back now towards those sheets I'm freed from. For the first time I am in the present entirely. It's love's logic Kline. How can you give yourself if you leave half of yourself behind?'

He left the room, though the voice was still purring 'Kline, Kline' behind him. His mother looked up, her face half expectancy, half fear.

'Is he . . . is he . . .?'

'You'll be happy together, Mother,' Kline said. 'Happier than you've ever been.'

'Oh, thank God . . . or, well I don't really mean that, do I? I'm sorry, that was . . . was it an occlusion?'

'No mother,' Kline said, 'that was a loop.'

5

It was Friday. Kline arrived in the sector around dusk. He spent some time as usual now walking through the ruined wharves. He could hear the voices clearly from the breaking-yard and see the ancient cargoes still strewn in the rubble. These days the sector smelt good to him. The haze no longer bothered his eyes.

He hadn't understood at first why you had to pay for everything, for food, sex, music, even for a conversation. His sister's friend had explained it to him one night. Time is money, she said, they had said it so often they had made it true. Now money was the key back into time.

It had been a source of much debate at the Centre, whether time could congeal in areas outside the wipings, and if so how potently. Some of his colleagues suspected there was a concentration of time in the sector, but no one greatly cared. It was seen as an area of contagion. The Flecks were famously diseased with custom and tradition.

He loved the greyness here. The rainbow stimuli that polychromed the city had started to hurt his eyes. In one of the films he'd tracked for memories a man had said, 'Life's in colour, but black and white's somehow more realistic.' He was beginning to understand what he meant. There were those who insisted ever more clamorously that time's stalling and reversal had been metonymically stated in the pattern of the names of St Petersburg. They claimed the sequence – Petersburg, Leningrad, Petersburg – was the symmetric arc for the reversal. Kline had been forming a library of sources. He felt honeycombed now that he was back in the sector.

The dead tenements would occasionally clatter as a Fleck lurched out of a doorway. Kline made for the spot by the water. Not that he could see much water, but the debris fascinated him. He sat and stared at the dolls with amputated limbs and the obsolescent wheels. A Fleck came stumbling along the wharf towards him and sat down. He held out his hand. Kline put a coin into it.

'Children's laughter excised. Fourth Dimension co-ordinates, and Beethoven slapping a saw in the forest. Riverrun past all past the past. Grey not colour of mourning. Smoke. Resurrection. Clothes lines signalling heaven. The machines wept. A radio once I had a radio once called Messiah.'

By now Kline was weeping with laughter and nodding. Back and forth he rolled on his haunches just like the Fleck himself was doing. He seemed so filled with his memories and his research he started to speak himself. The Fleck placed the coin back into his hand.

'The lepers of time kissing disinfected saints.

'Ennius was right. Once time has leeched through the mind, not even wiping can ever rinse it clear . . .' He was laughing again and the Fleck was laughing too. Here at the edge of the ruin. Dinosaur bones were scattered beneath them.

He walked slowly through the streets to the Little Rat. The dead ones that wanted to visit him did. He was courteous to all of them, though sometimes he found the old language hard, all those intonations and taxonomies.

He was accepted in the club at last, though they had thought at first he must be an agent. By dark he had already drunk five of the gins. His sister's friend was talking in his ear, old forbidden words, an antique syntax. Later they went upstairs. She opened the door. Perfume memories. A scent laid on a breeze beside a harbour, a thin cotton dress. The old sunshine he'd seen films of before the new weather: soaking through everything, bringing flowers from the ground, freckling children's noses. A hotel room overlooking the water. Dressing, undressing, promises of silk. Not his memories but staining him briefly. Silk lace-edged, holes tugged out of it by time, by the moths of time, leaving those minute loops to thread through. He bought more memories from her. A city with the lights bleeding across it.

In the morning she gave him the money back and asked him to talk about the dead. He told her about their strange manners and beautiful words.

The following week he was scanned for the first time in six months. The emergency lights went on and he was quarantined. Then interrogated for five days. They couldn't believe anyone in his position could choose such a partner and freely spend so much time in the sector. Technically he'd been wiped. He'd been documented as clear. They were convinced it was larger than him, that there must be a plot, that he was an infiltrator. Each time they hammered him with 'Why?' he only answered, 'Go ask my father. All understanding is now his.'

He was sentenced to ten years' labour in the Snow Sector. But long before the end of his sentence, like all the other prisoners there, he died.

Outside the Law

The old man stared out through the window at the rain. For fifty years he had stared out through this window at the same time each evening. At rain, sunshine, snow. He had stared out with children around this same table, eating and laughing and squabbling, and his wife in the kitchen shouting at them to keep quiet. Now he was alone here, for his wife was dead and the children gone. Except for the boy. Where was the boy? Late again, always late.

The boy was his grandchild. His daughter had been only sixteen when he was born. He would have gone for adoption, but the old man's wife wouldn't hear of it. So they had all stayed in the little house. Then one day the girl disappeared. And on another day, the darkest day of all, his wife had died. Now there were only him and the boy, but where was the boy?

When the little gate clinked and he came down the path at last, he was holding a handkerchief to his face. He let himself in and sat down at the table. He kept the handkerchief over his face.

'What's the matter, lad?'

Suddenly the boy started crying. He took the handkerchief away. That morning, when the old man had seen him go off to school, his nose had been thin and delicate, like a girl's nose, like his mother's nose. Now it was flattened and there were still traces of blood on his upper lip.

'What was it, rugby?' the old man said, but he knew it wasn't. The boy said nothing.

'Have you been to the hospital? Did they take you to see a doctor? Is that why you're so late home?'

The boy stood up and walked into the kitchen. He came back with a cup of water in his hand.

'It was Tony Jepps,' he said. 'He hit me in the face with an iron bar.'

'That little bugger from Carol Street? Right, I'm going up there now to see his father.'

'No, Grandad, you don't understand,' the boy said and sat back down at the table. 'It's no good talking to his father.'

The boy took gentle sips of the water and looked out through the window over towards the park.

'Well, come on, lad. Whatever it is, it can't be that bad, surely.'

'It can,' the boy said. Finally, he turned back and looked the old man in the eyes. 'I've been selling drugs. Out on the street. I owe them money. Jepps and his gang. This is a first warning. If I don't pay them, there'll be more and it will be worse.'

If his nose had not been broken, the boy would have

taken another slap across the face. The old man felt a strange sensation in his stomach. Drugs.

'What kind of drugs?' he said. 'The soft ones, I suppose, eh? The ones they said in the paper you don't go to prison for any more?'

'No, Grandad,' the boy said. 'Hard ones. Coke. Some heroin.'

'Where've you been selling all this?'

'Out there. On the streets out there. And in the park.'

'And where did you get it from in the first place?'

'Jepps and his mates.'

'How much money do you owe?'

'Five hundred pounds.'

'You owe five hundred pounds?'

'I've got till next Monday to pay.'

'How did you come to owe all that money?'

'I wasn't cutting the stuff properly. And I did some bad deals with people who didn't pay up.'

Five hundred pounds. That had been two months' pay for him, to feed and raise his family. All that was left of his family was sitting in front of him now. The young drug dealer.

'We're going to the police,' the old man said, starting to get up from the table. 'It's the only way. You'll be in trouble for a bit, but at least we'll get it all over with and out of the way.'

'No,' the boy said sharply, and the old man was genuinely surprised at the look of terror in his face. 'No, we can't go to the police.'

'Why not?'

'These people . . . Jepps and his gang. If you go to the police, they kill you.'

'They won't kill anybody,' the old man said, waving his arm towards the window. 'Don't be so bloody silly.'

'They killed Billy Friel.'

'Billy Friel? The boy they found on the railway line last year? Did you know about that? When the police came round here asking, and you didn't say anything? Did you know about it all the time?'

The boy nodded his head slowly.

'We all knew about it. And they'll kill me the same way. They don't care about the police, they're not frightened of them.'

The old man looked through the window again. The rain had cleared, but the sky was still grey and threatening.

'We'll take you to the hospital,' he said finally, going over slowly to get his overcoat and cap, 'and get you fixed up. Then tomorrow morning I'll go to the building society. I kept some savings there after your grandmother died. I'd always thought, if your mother could manage to sort herself out and get married . . . well, never mind that now. You'll give back the five hundred you owe them, and that'll be an end to it, lad, won't it?'

The boy said nothing.

Richard Dadd in Bedlam

The world awaited the tick of the geologist's hammer. All the days and years it had kept wombed inside it, like an agate's milky lines orbiting its crooked shiny brilliant heart, could at last come to term. The fossils started gently yawning. Meteoric stones fled back towards the stars. Riddled limestone caves were healed of vacancy. The cliffs, wrapped in a tall white blindfold, strode into the waves. And the flints at last forgave their ancient quarry. It was my father – not my true father, but the earthly impostor – who came with the hammer to rouse the mineral world to its millennium: Robert Dadd, apothecary, first curator of the Chatham and Rochester Literary and Philosophical Institution. Proprietor of the Commercial and Mathematical School. Lecturer in chemistry and geology. Preacher of the age of science and enlightenment.

I am calm today, seated silently in my grey dittos, gazing on my vivid companions, here in the male criminal wing of the Royal Bethlehem Hospital in St George's Fields. They'll let you call it Bethlehem or Bethlem, but not (unless you'd be restrained again) Bedlam. Still, that's what we call it in our hearts, and how the voices in the street endlessly baptise this screaming issue. Now the chains are gone which they fastened once around our arms and legs and necks; no longer are we displayed to the eyes of the town for their edification. But this is Bedlam still, though its masters and its warders have been kind to me, I who have often been so savagely unkind to others.

Bethlehem: a place I'd visited already and even made a picture of, a watercolour, near the Greek Convent of the Nativity of Christ. It was inside these walls that I finally perfected it. Bethlehem was finished inside Bedlam. That was the trip they say cost me my sanity. Those are the words of their language. I speak a different one: it was on that journey I was swallowed by the sun, when he had removed the veils of the sky from his nakedness and glory, and claimed me as his own. My brain has scorched with his light ever since. In the desert heat inside my skull, the scorpions mate. I record the fragile lines of music that their hairy legs make as they rub together.

Italy, Greece, Turkey. In Bodrum we visited the castle of St Peter and there sketched marble fragments from the tomb of Mausolus. See how antiquity can survive through the motions of one hand and eye. By now the sun would fall out of the sky in the evening, and be buried in the sea in minutes. Thence to Lycia, Cyprus, Beirut, Syria, Palestine. In Safed an old Jew was bent almost double in the synagogue, pondering the Kabbalistic mysteries and mumbling his litanies as though the years meant nothing, as though the years were no more than grains of dust gathering on his sandals. Tribesmen surrounded us in Jericho, one with a beard so infernally black, it would have made a hundred fine stiff brushes. Our dragomen dispelled their heat with a cascade of words. From Jaffa to Alexandria we were given passage on a ship named *Hecate*.

Then we travelled along the Nile, as though we were the limbs of Osiris once more, waiting to be gathered up. I drew each day as Thebes grew closer, and Sir Thomas fired away at crocodiles with his long gun. Later, as we moored near the temples of Luxor, we went up on deck one night to find the crew – Egyptian and Nubian – circling the desert sand, chorusing themselves into a frenzy, while one chanted passages from the Koran. They would collapse finally under the brilliant moon, some of them foaming. The very next day the sun started to claim me for his own. Osiris. Old god, father of all newer ones. And that's when the spirits were released to torment me.

Osiris held me in his own arms and burned himself into my mind and body like a living brand. Sunstroke, they said. Those are the words of their language: I speak a different one. Once he had burned away the dross that preceded him, and I had the mark of the god upon me, then the demons came to pleasure themselves, for they always follow the god about. I saw my own past, my counterfeit parentage, the years of lies, and I cut the mark from my forehead with a knife – the blotch they called a birthmark and I knew now was the devil's footprint as he had walked over me in my cradle. Blood rose up like molten lava.

In Rome I saw at last the Pope's true nature, and while he walked about before the abomination of St Peter's, I fingered the knife under my cloak. God knows it was sharp enough, but there were too many guards for my mission to be accomplished. Sir Thomas came to fear me, sensing the power that is at the centre of our heavens as it shone inside me. Once I caught him out on deck, dicing with Death for my soul. Death the cold, the calculating, was showing him her white and drooping breast, and her garter glittered with the stillborn milk of pearls. I could easily have killed him then, but the time had not yet come.

How fearsome can the rage of the atoms be? My father taught chemistry like one who has unlocked the secret room, like the high priest entering the Holy of Holies. (Moses owed everything to the Egyptians. Before Yahweh ever was, Osiris is.) I travelled alone back to London.

As the god commanded I lived on nothing but ale and eggs, scattering the shells about me on the floor as harbingers of life, the frail calcium walls that curve about the living genius. When they came for me, they found three hundred eggs, though this, like everything of true significance, was lost on them. Trinitarians! They wanted to lock me away, but my father would not hear of it, so he took me into his own care, my father who understood above all things that understanding was forgiveness. His omnicompetent smile. I entreated him to travel with me back to Cobham, where I had first set eyes on Titian and Tintoretto, where I had seen for the first time how much paint can love flesh. And as we travelled, I beseeched him to tell me what the world was made of and how it was constructed. He smiled the true and liberal smile of one who knows what is to be known, and started to explain things to me again, as though I might unaccountably have forgotten them − I who have never forgotten anything except the sound the tide makes when it laps the shore.

'Remember when you were young and I told you how there was no life without fire, how Prometheus had stolen fire from the gods, how fire comes from the sun, so all life comes also from the sun? Men had sought the secret of fire through the centuries, and long long before they understood it they knew how to make it. Men can usually do things before they understand what they are doing.

'Air they thought an element, something indivisible into any smaller components than itself. It was the great Lavoisier who discovered it was a composite. He dispensed with the imaginary − he got rid of phlogiston. He realised that when phosphorus burned it married the air. That was why the resulting acid was heavier than the original material before the fire. Up to that time, everyone had thought when something burned it merely fell apart, disintegrated into bits of something simpler. Now they came to understand that when it burned it became even more complex than before. Phosphoric acid is richer in complexity than phosphorus itself.

'Now, once we could understand oxygen we could understand fire, for at last we were separating the world into its true colours, and we started to build up our table of the elements. Now we could read for the first time the world's signature.'

His face had become bright by now, and I knew the source of that illumination. I know where the dead lights live. I watch them as they circle me each night. Osiris had taught me the secret of the hieroglyphs, and enough of his own tongue that I could understand him when he spoke. The demons wear masks of flesh and dress themselves in kindly laughter.

We ate at the Ship Inn that evening and I prevailed upon him to continue.

'Imagine, Richard, the shock the world felt to learn that the four fundamental elements acknowledged since antiquity, earth, water, fire and air, were in truth all compounds. Even water, that homogeneous and transparent substance, turns out to be a compound, an invisible complexity. The scientists had to learn to separate and measure, to see water but to discover deep at the heart of it hydrogen and oxygen. And fire was a process, an intermarriage between things of a dissimilar nature, a miscegenation breeding hybrids.'

The god was angry that what he had put together in such flames of love and hatred should be divorced in this way by men with glass flasks and retorts, holding up their paltry scales to the one great eye of the sun. And the evening sun now started to settle its gold rays on my father's affable features through the window, focusing at last. A walk outside, I suggested. Why not a gentle stroll amongst those signatures?

'Geology is simply another way of reading the matter at hand,' my father continued as we walked. 'Many of the formations about here originate in the cretaceous period. The surfaces of earth are like ancient languages' – he actually said this, as though I still needed any further sign – 'waiting for us to come and decode them. We are surrounded by the mute script of the inanimate world.'

Inanimate! Not a diplomatic word to use before a mighty god and his creation. I took the spring knife from my pocket and jumped upon my father. No Richard, no, he shouted, fear lighting his eyes finally with the one true flame. Their greatest disguise is kindness. The old man was stronger than I had expected, though, and protected his throat with some vigour. It was the throat I was directed to, for I had already made countless drawings of all my relatives with their throats cut, opened for the spirit to enter, but despite my clawing and my kicking and my slaps I could not release his grasp. And so, failing my instructions in this one respect, I merely stabbed and stabbed and stabbed again. Stomach, groin, breast, thigh. The blade plunged and the wounds spurted, then another patch of flesh appeared for severing, and all the time his whimpering entreaties. No, Richard, no. Arteries gushed like little crimson springs. I could smell the sweetness of his blood upon me. Then he who had tried to steal the name of father finally lay still, with no more words tripping from his tongue. The sun licked his new red trophies and fell silent too.

From thence to France, where my razor nearly did find a throat to enter. And then asylum years began. Which, they tell me, will not end, for it seems that I must leave here dressed in pinewood.

I try to explain to the doctor, but he has an omnicompetent smile too and cannot see them all around as I can. Sometimes tiny, sometimes huge. They can block out the whole sky at night or creep like bacteria with shrivelled wings into the orifices of your own body, waiting there, preparing the machines of torture. My visitations.

Intermittently the pharmacopoeia: they sink a rainbow in your blood and dry out for one afternoon the ceaseless grieving drizzle in your soul.

They are filing out now to the green yards, but today I shall stay here. I lift this tiny brush and permit my hand to make the immense journey through the air towards the picture. Already that lady's breasts are huge and pointing to a different purpose than the one she keeps her face for. There is a gigantic calcium deception trapped inside her bodice. Already the patriarch is half-blind with the shadows of his years. I painted so often the figures of that lost time of translation in the forest, with Oberon and Titania: so quick bright things come to confusion. They turn the witching night to tinsel for their window decorations.

The daisies' brilliant faces are exploding into wisdom. Watch now as the fairy feller brings his axe down on the hazelnut. If he splits it the first time, how many new worlds do you think will fly out? And am I to be left here alone again to witness them?